CW01096062

The Executioners

The Executioners

A 'Simon Shard' novel

Philip McCutchan

HODDER AND STOUGHTON
LONDON SYDNEY AUCKLAND TORONTO

British Library Cataloguing in Publication Data
McCutchan, Philip
  The executioners: a Simon Shard novel.
  I. Title
  823'.914[F]   PR6063.A167

ISBN 0 340 34446 6

Hodder and Stoughton Editorial Office: 47 Bedford Square, London WC1B 3DP.

1

They – Whitehall, the media, France and so on – were calling it a mini summit, presumably because although President Ligot of France, the host country, would open the first session, the heads of state were not taking part themselves. But it was going to be big: in Paris the NATO and EEC brass were due shortly to meet their counterparts in the Soviet Bloc. The Russian Foreign Minister was coming, with a lot of the usual grim-faced officials and security men, plus men from Poland, East Germany, Czechoslovakia, Hungary. The British Foreign Minister was going to have a difficult role to play; the French Government wanted a closer link with the Iron Curtain countries by way of trade, sharing of resources, and some sort of arms deal. The British Government did not, less so did Washington. They all wanted to ease the tension between East and West and that was all. No firm matiness, no unilateral sacrifices, plenty of wariness, and a tightrope to be walked by the British delegation who would be in close scramble line telephonic communication with the Prime Minister, known basically to view the whole thing with the utmost suspicion. The Foreign Secretary knew quite well that his job was on the line if he boobed in the very smallest degree. The knowledge wasn't going to help him when he got to France and the fanfare of trumpets and the French guard of honour in full dress with band. The Prime Minister could be a very tough nut when crossed.

And there could be a link, as Shard knew, with what was happening today.

It was a day of stifling heat; London was hell, Heathrow several degrees worse. Shard sweltered, his shirt collar damp and clinging. So much pouring sweat that he almost feared the effect on the Continental 7.65 mm automatic in his shoulder holster. With men from the special FO security section posted around, he had moved through the airport buildings behind the Russians, a departing Kremlin trade mission being given the VIP treatment en route for home and austerity. August: the holiday season in full swing, and the place littered with baggage and people, white, black, yellow or merely with a tan. A kind of bedlam, and the lounges and cafeteria filthy as usual, unable to cope with mass muckiness. Britain's front door, out and home, the knocker never polished, highly unimpressive but expressive of the inhabitants and possibly not much worse than was to be found in a number of other countries . . .

Shard caught the eye of a man from the Yard: the Met had naturally been fully informed and was maintaining an eye, since Heathrow was part of their patch, but in fact this was to be a Foreign Office job, Shard's job. Stanislav Asipov might or might not be important: time would tell. But Russian trade missions were often enough cover for something rather more lethal; and three days ago Stanislav Asipov had made a break for freedom, speeding out from a big Marks and Spencers' branch in the Midlands during a courtesy tour. The freedom hadn't lasted; sour-faced men, blank-looking persons in dark suits and hats, had chased and caught, and Asipov, white and frightened, had been marched back to his comrades. Now Whitehall wanted to know what was going on. The British Government didn't like virtual kidnap on its sovereign territory and Moscow didn't normally make such overt pounces. Hedge, Shard's boss, had been beside himself with worry just because of the forthcoming Paris jaunt; there could be that link. Hedge had been so agitated that he had spilled a cup of Foreign Office coffee over a new suit and had managed to find a way of blaming Shard for it.

Shard paused to light a cigarette; the man from the Yard drifted past. A detective inspector from the Diplomatic Protection Group: Shard, in his Yard days, had known him as a DC when he himself had been a newly-promoted detective superintendent.

"Just gone into the VIP lounge, sir," the Yard man murmured.

"Right. Pass the word through. I'll be down."

The Yard man sauntered on. Shard drew smoke down deep, blew out a dull brown cloud. He really ought to give up: he inhaled too much. But at times smoking was an occupational hazard, and in spite of it he was fit enough, hard enough. If he didn't smoke he might eat too much and then his leanness would be replaced by the unhandy weight of a gut, which was much more of a drag on NHS resources than was smoking. Without paying the earth, you couldn't get a meal without chips, the downfall of fit manhood. Look around you these days, and all you saw was fat. Fat young men with chip-fed stomachs that drooped over their trouser tops like sacks of flour, fatter middle-aged men, gross old ones, fat, doughy faces and pudgy arms, horrible adverts for the omnipotent chip pan. Ban chips and the race might survive to be fried in its turn by the next nuclear holocaust.

As always, nuclear holocausts and Russia went together in men's minds.

Shard made his way, not hurrying, to an area where the general public was not admitted: down to the apron, where the Aeroflot jet stood ready to embark its passengers. A chartered aircraft, not a service flight, specially laid on for the trade delegation.

As he walked out onto the concrete he was met by another plain clothes man: one of his own this time – Detective Sergeant Kenwood.

"All right, Harry?"

"Yes, sir."

"No mistakes. Right man first time."

Kenwood gave a brief grin. "Photo imprinted on my memory, sir!"

Shard nodded; he carried a similar imprint in his mind, but the Russians were never fools and disguise was easy enough. So you didn't go by the face; you went by the build, the walk, the carriage. He and Harry Kenwood had been shown film taken discreetly of the Russians while they had been cavorting around factories all over Britain – South Wales, Birmingham, Sheffield, Wolverhampton, Newcastle, Glasgow, Glenrothes. Just a simple, routine precaution with nothing specific in mind but this time it had paid off. Or it might – in the end – *not* pay off. Stanislav Asipov might turn out to be of no importance at all, and never mind what Whitehall had thought. In that case, there were going to be some red faces around the elegant corridors of state. Important or not, Moscow wasn't going to like what was about to happen and it would be pointless to upset them over nothing.

Shard moved to an unmarked car and bent for a word with the driver. Inside, in addition to the driver, were three plain clothes officers from Shard's section, all armed but under strict orders not to show their weapons unless Shard gave the signal. Also in the area were other officers, disguised as airport workers, looking disinterested but nevertheless ready. Shard did not, in fact, expect much physical difficulty: the Aeroflot was right inside British territory and geographically a long way from take-off. The difficulty would be verbal. In point of fact Hedge, Shard's immediate boss, had been adamant that there was to be no discussion. Do, he had said, don't talk. Nip any talk in the bud, smartly. A fast grab and away. That was what Whitehall wanted. The talk would come later.

"Easier said than done," Shard had pointed out unoriginally. "The Russians aren't going to part in silence, Hedge."

Hedge had flapped a hand. "Up to you," he'd said distantly. "You're a Detective Chief Superintendent, you should know how to cope."

"Yes, Hedge," Shard had answered politely, and added, "How would you cope?"

"I dislike being asked to teach people their jobs."

That had been that. Shard, who never needed Hedge's tuition, had divined the pearl that lay behind the snapped words: Hedge had no idea how he would cope. Hedge wasn't a field man any more, he belonged strictly to the backroom. He was happy there. It was safer and more comfortable and if things went wrong he could always shift the blame. That was why he was never too precise unless, as on this occasion, he'd had his orders from above. When that was so, the abode of blame was crystal clear and he had no worries; but he wouldn't commit himself to the details of the work-out even so. Not his job. Fair enough – it wasn't. But Shard, still basically a copper, was feeling a shade sunk in the depths of the diplomatic scene, the more so as a highly-placed official from the Russian Embassy was seeing the trade delegation off. And *he* wasn't going to remain tongue-tied when the plain clothes men went in for the grab.

Moving back from the unmarked car, Shard glanced at his watch: five more minutes if the schedule was kept to and the Russians didn't overdo the departure conviviality. One or two of them had done just that, during factory lunches, and had been propped up by their security men, carried out like zombies to the waiting motorcade and thrust inside to blear their way back to base through the British countryside.

But this time they were prompt.

On the dot, they began coming out onto the apron, forty-seven of trade delegation plus obvious guards, twelve in number. Mostly squat and square, mostly unsmiling, they filed towards the waiting jet. Shard and Kenwood watched closely: there seemed to be no face that tallied with Stanislav Asipov. Shard's guess looked as though it had been spot on: some facial distortion, just in case. The British – and how right, this time, the Russians were – could never be trusted. All the same, they hadn't been very clever. They'd given the game away from the word go. One of the delegates was being propped up by two security men. He didn't look drunk; he looked drugged. His feet scraped the concrete as he was propelled along and although he didn't look like Asipov's photograph the build fitted. A pity he wasn't walking, but Shard was convinced he was Asipov. The build apart – he was just a little taller and less square than his mates – the Russians hadn't in fact done a very good job in altering the outline of the face. That became obvious as the distance closed.

Shard glanced at Harry. "The invalid one. Check?"

Kenwood nodded.

Shard glanced over his shoulder, left, lifted an eyebrow

towards the unmarked car. The plain clothes men got out in a bunch. Shard indicated their quarry and they moved fast. Joined by Harry Kenwood, two officers approached each of the guards supporting Asipov. Shard went forward, right hand inside his double-breasted jacket.

"Just a moment," he said.

For a few seconds there was a silence. Then more bedlam was added to the inferno of Heathrow. Through it, over it, Shard shouted that he had reason to believe kidnap was being attempted.

★   ★   ★

Hedge wrung his hands. "You should never have said that, Shard."

"There had to be a given reason."

"No there hadn't. I made the very point! *No talking*." Hedge stormed up and down his office, two tall windows, opulent desk, hat-stand, thick carpet all over in indication of his standing in the Foreign Office hierarchy. "Once a policeman, always a policeman. *Whatever you say may be taken down in evidence* . . . God help us all! No imagination, no initiative." He paced on, like a pudgy panther. Shard waited for the fury to subside. To some extent, it did. Hedge went on, sounding plaintive now, "I've had the Minister of State on the line. There's already been a complaint from the Soviet Embassy, Shard!"

"Did you expect there wouldn't be?"

"Yes – no – oh, don't be so impertinent, Shard. I say again, the word kidnap should never have been mentioned at all. They're making a lot of that as one would expect. Kidnap! It's – it's *insulting*." Hedge brought out a silk handkerchief and dabbed at his wobbling cheeks. "They say a country can't be said to kidnap one of its own people in a foreign land. He was sick – Asipov was. A sick man who wanted to go home to Russia where he has a wife and family. That's what they said."

"It wasn't what Asipov said."

"Oh? What did he say, then?"

Shard said, "Mostly Russian but a few words in English. 'I want to stay,' he said."

Hedge looked a shade better. "Well, of course, that's something. I understand there were fisticuffs. Is that so?"

"Yes," Shard answered briefly.

"A pity – "

"Unavoidable, if the orders were to be carried out." Shard was angry: his jaw still felt as though it had been dislocated, and Kenwood had a black eye. "I suggest you report as much to the Foreign Secretary."

Hedge seemed to stiffen to attention at the mere mention of his God. Shard had the feeling that he was about to be accused of sacrilege, of taking names in vain. But all Hedge said was, "I shall report, of course. The next thing's Asipov himself."

"An interrogation?"

"When possible, yes. When the doctors say so . . . he's been taken to Westminster Hospital, under guard of course. Held incommunicado."

"I know that," Shard said pointedly. Hedge didn't comment; his attention was being directed elsewhere. There was a loud buzzing sound and he was looking agitated, staring at one of his windows.

He said, "Ring for my secretary, Shard. Tell her to bring the fly-killer. I believe it's a bluebottle. Nasty things, bluebottles. Absolutely crammed with disease germs." Then he went back to business. "Your French assignment, Shard. I may take you off it."

Shard raised an eyebrow. "Is the Foreign Secretary not going – because of this new business with Asipov?"

"He's still going, but you may not. You're going to be needed here now, for a while at any rate."

"If I don't go who will?"

"I don't know yet," Hedge said. Then he flipped a fat hand, dismissingly. "That's all for now, Shard. I'm sure you have things to see to. I'll let you know when Asipov's available – in the meantime, keep yourself handy. No going home until I say so."

Shard left the room as Hedge's secretary came in armed with the fly-killer; Miss Fleece had a predatory gleam in her eye as though she liked killing bluebottles, the act of pursuit bringing some excitement to her daily routine of files and telephones. Shard went down to the security section, which was housed in the basement. He would not be sorry if he missed the Paris assignment; personal guard duties were not much in his line, but the Foreign Secretary, being a bigwig, needed a senior man in charge of the security arrangements. Paris was a hot spot these days, with blowings-up happening all the time, and there was to be a drive through the city in company with the French President – purely in his capacity as host – and a lot of brass from both NATO and the EEC. A real get-together, and such assignments were misery for the minions; long hours, a lot of hanging about, boring speeches and too much food – either that, or none at all if events so dictated. Always difficulty in finding an opportunity to pee, and standing guard when your VIP had found *his* opportunity. Inspection of the loo first – a bomb could always have been planted in the cistern and you were duty bound not to trust the hosts.

Shard chatted with Harry Kenwood, whose eye was darkening fast. Kenwood told him that his Detective Inspector had just gone off sick: his car had been run into from behind and he'd had no head restraint. Result, a badly ricked neck that had left him with a sideways slant and a good deal of pain. A fine time to choose, Shard thought, but it couldn't be helped. The DI would be in plaster for a long while; something wrong with his back as well, Kenwood said gloomily, he might even be on traction. With a number of other matters on their plate currently, they were going to be a little thin on the ground command-wise if anything else happened to blow.

★   ★   ★

The call to Westminster Hospital didn't come in until late that afternoon, by which time Shard had been busy recapping such as was known about Stanislav Asipov. The Russian, whose first visit to Britain this was believed to be, was in charge of a project concerned with the supply of natural gas – something similar to the pipeline that had caused such anguish to the American Government back in 1982, but not on this occasion being anything to do with the piping of gas through to the EEC. It was purely domestic to the Eastern Bloc countries and Asipov had come over to study British techniques and also to acquire some British materials. His loyalty had never been in question; he was known to be a good communist, a hard worker at his job and for the party, a family man with a wife and three children, two boys and a girl, plus an aged widowed mother living in Kharkov, which was his own home town. Asipov was thirty-nine years old, was an asthmatic, a non-smoker because of this, and a non-drinker on the grounds that alcohol impaired efficiency and his life was devoted to working for Russia. The Moscow authorities would have been grieved to learn that so much information was available in Britain, but there were always ways and means of acquiring knowledge when necessary and they might have suspected it. There was a good deal more detail, all of which Shard committed to memory, since a full personal knowledge of a man was of immense value in interrogation and when the subject got the idea that all was an open book he was usually inclined to let go the guard on his tongue. Or if not usually, then often enough. It was a line to be followed in any case.

Asipov was lying in bed in a private room and the guard was strong: no less than four plain clothes men provided by the Yard, all armed. There was a nurse at the bedside, and Shard was met at the door by a doctor.

"I understand he's fit for questioning," Shard said.

"Right – up to a point."

"What does that mean, Doctor?"

"It means I've had my arm twisted. He's not well – you'll see that for yourself. But someone in Whitehall has spoken, as if I need to tell you. Don't press him too far, though."

"I won't," Shard promised. They wanted a live Asipov, not a dead one, and the doctor's tone was grave. "What's the matter with him?"

The doctor said, "We don't know. He's doped – we don't know what with. It's something new – new in this country, at any rate. His mind seems clear enough, but there's a degree of paralysis of the muscles, plus wasting."

13

"Wasting?"

"Yes. I don't understand it unless he's been under this drug for a long while, which I gather he can't have been – all that gallivanting around the country with his delegation, he'd have had to be fit and mobile for that, obviously – "

"So it's a fast acting drug?"

The doctor nodded. "I think so, yes. That's the only answer. In non-technical terms, that is. It's not so much fast *acting* really as fast in its effects, which is something different. It's *speeded up* the wasting process, that's what I mean."

"And the prognosis?"

"I really can't say, not knowing what the drug is. But if the wasting goes on, well, then I wouldn't say his chances were particularly good."

Shard nodded and went into the room. He said he would prefer to be alone with Asipov. The nurse glanced at the doctor, who gave a dubious nod, and she left, as did the doctor. The door was closed; the four-man guard waited outside. Shard sat by the bed and looked down at the Russian. The man's eyes were flickering about the room and his tongue came out to lick dry-looking lips, and the legs shifted a little, shifted stiffly as though the effort was a large one, beneath the sheet. There was no other movement.

Shard made himself known. "I'm Detective Chief Superintendent Shard, attached Foreign Office. I know you as Stanislav Asipov of the trade delegation from Moscow. Is that correct?"

"It is correct," Asipov said in a weak voice.

"And you speak some English."

"A little."

"Then I'm going to ask you some questions," Shard said. "It's in your own interest to answer them as fully as you can. I'm here to help. First, do you confirm that you want to ask for asylum here in Britain?"

"Yes, I wish to stay."

"Will you tell me why?"

"Because there is here a better life." The voice seemed weaker already; it was an effort to speak at all. Shard felt disinclined to press; his was merely a preliminary investigation, the diplomatic interrogation in depth would be made later by the Foreign Office backroom boys, the ones with special knowledge of the Eastern Bloc and its devious politics and the undercurrents of interplay between East and West. If he pressed too far now, Shard thought, he might send the man over the brink. Nevertheless, there were things he had to establish.

He said, "Because there is a better life. Is that all, Comrade Asipov?" There was no response and he tried again. "What about your wife, your three children, and your mother in Kharkov? Will you willingly leave them all behind, to face whatever the men in Moscow make them face because of your defection? Will you risk their lives for a better life for yourself . . . or is there some other reason?"

The lips moved but he couldn't hear the voice. He bent closer, straining to catch anything that might emerge. There was beseechment in the eyes. Then there was a knock on the door, a peremptory sound. Shard, cursing to himself, got to his feet and went to the door. He jerked it open.

"Well?"

One of the Yard men said, "Message from the FO, Mr Shard. You're wanted back at once. Urgent. A Mr Hedge. You're to stop the interrogation."

"No reason given?"

"None, sir."

★ ★ ★

Hedge had been shaken rigid; there had been a call said to be from a member of the staff of the Soviet Embassy. If this was true, whoever was on the line had not been phoning from the Embassy. The call had been from a public call-box. And most worrying of all, the caller had asked for Hedge in person. Hedge had had the call put through and a voice had said, "The man in hospital will die if he is not returned, not handed back. He is drugged . . . there is an antidote and this antidote is known only to certain persons. You will be contacted again very soon."

15

In a high voice Hedge had asked, "How long before he dies?"

"You have two days from now," the caller said, and hung up. Hedge jigged the receiver-rest, uselessly, then banged the thing down and mopped at his face. When Shard reported, Hedge gave him the bare facts.

"So what do you do now?" Shard asked.

"It's out of my hands," Hedge said, looking on the verge of blind panic. "A Prime Ministerial decision, I would say. What worries me is that the caller – a man, obviously a Russian – used my name. Hedge." He added this because Hedge was not in fact his real name. Hedge was a pseudonym descriptive of his job, which was to act as a hedge or screen between the Head of Security and lesser men, which included even Scotland Yard. His real name was never spoken, was not even known, something to do with his past service. "There's been the most appalling leak in security, Shard!"

"We'll take that as read, Hedge. The first point is, who was the man? You said he didn't use the Embassy phone. How do we know he's genuine? The answer is – we don't, do we, Hedge?"

Hedge gave him a blank look. "What are you suggesting, Shard?"

"This: that we take no notice of that call – until the next one comes. In the meantime – "

"What if the man dies, simply because we didn't hand him back to where he belongs? What's the press going to make of that, what's Moscow going to make of it?"

Shard said drily, "Capital, I would say. But we've not got that far yet. You said we have two days. We'd better use them, Hedge. Put on the full works to find out what makes Asipov tick. I didn't get much out of him if anything, but I did get the idea there's more behind his defection than a simple wish for the capitalist way of life. And the Russians seem very anxious to get him back – right?"

Hedge nodded, blew out a long breath. "Oh dear, oh dear, what a bother all this is, Shard! I'll have to let H of S know, of course, and no doubt he'll decide. In the meantime, we must drop our own interrogation – yours, that is. Policemen can be clumsy – no offence, of course, Shard, nothing personal – "

16

"Of course not. I do understand, Hedge."

"Yes, good. I'll get the experts onto him if H of S approves." Hedge reached out for one of his telephones; the Head of Security was still in his office, a more palatial one even than Hedge's, a whole suite including a bedroom while Hedge just had a cloakroom with facilities. As his hand touched the internal phone the outside line burred at him, the closed line used by the Yard, the Cabinet Office and Number Ten.

"Damn," Hedge said irritably. The caller was Hesseltine, Assistant Commissioner Crime, Hedge's *bête noire*. Such a rude man, and impatient, never knew his place.

"What do you want?" Hedge snapped down the line. "I'm busy, you know – "

"A moment of your valuable time, Hedge. It's important, or I think so. A woman's come in – "

"*What* woman?"

"You'll see. I'm taking the liberty of having her brought over to you. There's an Asipov connection. And France comes into the picture. Remember the Foreign Secretary's visit, Hedge?"

2

Waiting for Hesseltine's mysterious woman to turn up, Hedge made his internal call to the Head of Security. The wheels were set in motion, the wheels that would dig out Stanislav Asipov's deepest secrets – or would try to. Shard's guess was that the Russian defector wouldn't say anything that might add to the burdens about to be placed on his family in Kharkov. Hedge went into the ethics of allowing a man to die: the ethics, that was, from his, Hedge's, viewpoint.

"It's going to be immensely difficult, Shard. I don't know how we can justify it, really. The blasted press . . . after all, the man's a Russian – "

"Who's asking for asylum. If he goes back, he's not going to be popular. One form of death may be as good as another for all we know."

Sagely, Hedge nodded. "Well, yes, there is that."

Shard studied the heavy, fleshy face. Hedge was looking better; he was always an easy man to drag from depression, it was simply a case of finding the right phrase, one that he could trot out as his own later on in justification for his baser deeds. For his part Shard saw it as fairly base to let a man die when he didn't have to, but he could appreciate the importance of getting Asipov to talk . . . maybe he was getting inured to nastiness, though he hoped he wasn't. Danger was one thing, dirty tricks another. Largely he detested the Foreign Office and all that, deep down, it stood for. Intrigue, double talk, blatant lies however blandly uttered – though all, of course, for a noble cause, national security. It didn't do to think too much about it; just get on with the job. And what he had just said to Hedge was absolutely true: Asipov might well face the bleakest of futures if he was

18

handed back to Moscow and death in Britain might be more appealing.

Miss Fleece came in to say the ACC was waiting.

"Hesseltine's come himself?" Hedge looked disagreeable; he reached into a drawer of his desk and brought out a packet of Rennie's. Two tablets went into his cheeks, to be slowly absorbed in his spittle. "Oh, all right, Miss Fleece. Send him in."

Hesseltine entered, accompanied by the woman, whom he introduced as Ernestine Kolnisenko. She didn't look Russian and she wasn't, she was English, married to a Russian, now dead. She was a stringy woman with a reddish nose that carried a drip at the end. She looked the picture of misery but there was hope in her eyes that such an important man as Hedge might lift her from her woes. Her voice, which once started was hard to stop, was like her name: earnest.

She said, "Mr Hesseltine's been so kind. It's so good of you to see me. I – "

"I understand," Hedge broke in, bringing her to the point, "that you have some connection with . . . er, current events?"

"Yes," she said. "I happened to be at Heathrow this morning, I was seeing a cousin off to America, you see, quite an elderly cousin, a cousin of my mother's as a matter of fact – "

"And?"

"And?" She gawped back at Hedge, apparently thrown off her stroke by being interrupted in full flow.

Hedge said irritably, "What happened at Heathrow, Mrs – er – "

"Kolnisenko. Mrs Kolnisenko." She repeated the name slowly, syllable by syllable, to make sure he got it right.

"Yes, yes, yes."

She took a deep breath, gearing herself up. "I saw what happened. Some of it, that is. I saw a man being taken away and some Russians making a fuss about it." She looked at Shard. "I saw this gentleman too as a matter of fact, I recognised him the moment I walked in here and I said to myself, well, that's a bit of luck because he'll be able – "

"Yes, yes!"

"Well, you see, the point is really, I recognised the man. The other man. The one they were taking away. Stanislav Asipov. I'll never forget him, never, and anyway I have a good memory for faces. It was Asipov who was responsible for Ivan's, that's my late husband's, death."

She stopped there, the drip growing worse. She brought out a handkerchief and blew her nose. Her eyes were very red and there was a haunted look. It appeared she had loved Ivan Kolnisenko; she began to hiccup and Hedge, in a tizzy to get her going again now, rang for Miss Fleece to bring a glass of water. This failed to do the trick and the hiccups continued spasmodically for a while. Through them, the story emerged. Dead Ivan had worked with Asipov for about fifteen years and had worked well; Asipov had grown jealous of the regard in which Ivan Kolnisenko had been held and five years ago had trumped up charges of disloyalty against him, disloyalty to the party, and Ivan's fate had been sealed. No notice was taken of his protestations of innocence and he had been despatched to Siberia, whence news had come after six months that he had died. Well, Ernestine Kolnisenko said bravely, that was water under the bridge now. It was her son she was bothered about, her son Mikhail, now aged twenty and still in Russia.

"And you?" Hedge asked keenly. "How long is it since you left Russia, Mrs Kolnisenko?"

She said, "I left soon after I got the news about Ivan's death – "

"They let you leave?"

"After a bit of bother," she said. "I was interrogated and that and then suddenly they said I could go. After all, I was British by birth. But I wasn't allowed to take Mikhail."

"That must have been a wrench, surely?"

She seemed to ponder. "Yes and no," she said after a while, frowning. "Mikhail was very Russian and he hated anything to do with Britain, not that he'd ever been here, but you know what it's like when you're half British but surrounded by Russians, don't you, and then he never did believe his father was innocent. He thought I'd suborned Ivan, you see, me being British. Well, that I couldn't take and I wanted so desperately to get back home, home being England with my mother and dad. They were old, you see, and they needed me. So I settled for what I'd been offered and I came back. But now . . . well, I never did wish any harm to Mikhail, of course I didn't, he's my own flesh and blood all said and done, and now I'm so worried I don't know what to do, really I don't, Mr Hedge."

She stopped again, like a tap, and sat with her hands folded in her lap, gazing hopefully at salvation. Hedge coughed and cleared his throat importantly; he had always liked adulation. He said, "Yes. Yes, I understand, and I shall do all I can to help. Can you be more precise? About your worry, I mean. D'you believe the Russians will in some way connect your son with the man Asipov, who was responsible for his father's imprisonment?"

"And death," she said with emphasis.

"Oh yes, and death."

"No," she said and, astonishingly, laughed. "Well, I mean! How could they? It just doesn't tie up."

Hedge reddened angrily and fidgeted with his blotter. "What, then?"

She said, "It's what the UFO people told me, you see. One of them came over from France – "

"UFO?" Hedge seemed rocked, as well, Shard thought, he might. There was an air of the ludicrous about Ernestine Kolnisenko without bringing in the Unidentified Flying Objects, if that was indeed what she was referring to. Shard racked his brains for some terrorist organisation that might call themselves the UFO but failed to find one. And it was in fact the Unidentified Flying Objects that the woman had in mind.

She went on, "They're hippies really, living in a commune in France. In where was it . . . the Ardeech, that's it – "

"Ardèche?"

"Yes. They come from all over – here, France, Spain, lots of places including Russia apparently. They believe funny things so this young girl said – "

21

"What young girl?" Hedge's mind was in a whirl by this time; Shard, glancing at Hesseltine, caught the ACC's sardonic look. He'd heard it all already and was enjoying the sight of Hedge's face.

Mrs Kolnisenko said, "Well, she's known as little fat Annie. That was all she told me, or rather her friend did. There were two of them, you see, her and a boy, I never did get to know his name. French, he was. This little fat Annie was Russian. She had an exit permit as one of some sort of cultural tour, I think, and she'd left the tour and gone hippie. Defected, like. Anyway, the point is, she knew Mikhail . . . he'd given her my address here before she left Russia, said he wanted to get in touch but couldn't off his own bat. And that's what worries me, you see, Mr Hedge."She leaned forward, red eyes beseeching. "Mikhail's right out of contact – "

"With you? Surely that's – "

"No," she said passionately. "I mean yes, with me too, but with *life* as well. There was a mix-up, you see. According to this little fat Annie, Mikhail was working in a steel foundry in Volgograd . . . he went on a binge one night – this was last year – got drunk on vodka. Out for four days and didn't go home. Well, in the meantime a man of the same name as him, another Mikhail Kolnisenko at the steel works, fell into a vat or something of molten steel – and they thought it was my boy. Then there was this mix-up – "

Hedge interrupted, "Really I don't see how they could make such a mistake, Mrs – "

"It can happen," she said, still passionate, "in Russia. You'd never *believe* the inefficiency and the way everything depends on forms. It's all forms and passes, all bits of paper. Literally, you can't live without it, without paper proof that you're alive. Internal passports . . . look, Mikhail was living with a family in Volgograd, and they were called, not that there were any remains. They were told to bring my boy's internal passport, which they did. It was stamped deceased and that was that. When the real Mikhail turned up, it was too late. After that – well, without an internal passport you just don't exist, I daresay you know that."

Hedge nodded and tried to get a word in but the woman went on regardless. "You can't do anything. Can't withdraw savings, collect parcels and that at the post office, move house, arrange a holiday, even get a job – specially can't get a job. You do see what I mean, don't you, Mr Hedge? He might as well be dead. In a sense he is. He's just not recognised as existing, no-one takes a blind bit of notice, not because they can't see him standing there when he goes to the bureau to say he's alive, but because his internal passport says deceased and they have to believe it. I know it sounds daft, but that's Russia for you. My boy, well, best way of putting it is, he's sort of . . . *un*dead. Not *dead*, but . . . I mean, there he is, he walks around, you can touch him, talk to him, but without that internal passport – "

"Yes, yes, yes, I do know – "

She went on as regardless as before. "Without that, no-one is allowed to believe he exists because officially he *doesn't*. It's not that they don't *know* who he is, but they can't admit it. Little fat Annie, she said he's become a non-person. That's what he wanted me to know, you see. I asked myself *why* . . . well, it's obvious he wants help in some way, isn't it? I've been wondering . . . maybe he's so fed up with Russia and non-life that he's going to do something dangerous, something against Russia. Like trying to get out of the country under cover, you know what I mean?" She hesitated. "I was wondering if there was anything you could do, Mr Hedge. He probably expects that. After all, he's half British."

Hedge was flummoxed and angry: he was concerned with Asipov, not with this wretched woman and her non-person son; they failed to interest him and he resented being used as some kind of means of re-establishment, or resurrection, of the undead. That was not his brief. In any case, half British wasn't good enough for the FO to raise any questions with the Russians, who would naturally claim the wretched boy as their own, and never mind what the fellow 'probably expected'. What could he do? He temporised. He asked, "Would your son consider asking to be allowed to join you in Britain, Mrs Kolnisenko?"

"He *can't ask*, Mr Hedge! They wouldn't listen. He doesn't exist. If you don't exist you can't emigrate, can you?"

"I suppose not." Hedge drummed his fingers on his desk and puffed out his cheeks. He brought the conversation back to Stanislav Asipov by asking, "Do you believe Asipov would help – if he was back in Russia, that is – is that it?"

"Is he going back to Russia? From that scene – "

"I can't comment on that," Hedge said hastily. "I'd be obliged if you'd answer my question, Mrs Kolnisenko."

She said, "Yes, he might."

Hedge was surprised; his question had been directed towards prising out some information, if any was to be had, about Asipov, something that might prove useful in the interrogation of the defector. Now, he found two things astonishing: one, that the help of a discredited defector should be seen as likely to be of use to anyone; and two, that the woman should think help might be forthcoming from the very source that had been responsible for laying false information against Mikhail's father. He asked curiously, "Why should you think that, Mrs Kolnisenko?"

"I don't see why not. *In the circumstances.*"

"The circumstances?"

"Yes." The bony face was slightly flushed now and there was a defensive look. Shard had a strong feeling that some underlying pearl of truth was about to emerge and he also had a suspicion what that pearl might be, and he was right. Ernestine Kolnisenko didn't quite belong to the permissive society but twenty odd years ago, as it turned out in the next few minutes, she had been permissive with Stanislav Asipov, her husband's boss, and Mikhail was the fruit of the liaison. And it had not been jealousy of the sort initially postulated by Ernestine that had led to the false charge against Ivan Kolnisenko. Ivan had brooded over a strong likeness between Mikhail and Stanislav Asipov and there had in any case been other reasons for his developing suspicion. One day, beside himself, he had gone to Asipov and had threatened to kill him. Asipov had got out from under and had thereafter acted in self defence, had shopped Kolnisenko on that false information, and

Kolnisenko's protestations of cuckoldry had been disregarded by the prosecution at the trial, held in secret. Mikhail had no idea that he was the son of Stanislav Asipov.

"Are *you* quite certain he is Asipov's son?" Hedge asked.

"Well, I should be, Mr Hedge. It was Stanislav who – "

"Yes, yes, quite. I understand that. But your husband. Presumably he – er – "

"No, " she said very firmly. "Ivan couldn't get it up, hadn't been able to for years. He always knew Mikhail wasn't his."

Hedge was scarlet.

★   ★   ★

Hesseltine had kept silent throughout, but after the woman had gone he gave Hedge and Shard the details of the hippie commune in the Ardèche department of France. They were all crazy, the ACC said, bonkers. Drugs were largely responsible, according to little fat Annie via Ernestine Kolnisenko, for what Hesseltine called the hippies' suspension of disbelief. It was a religious thing – of a sort, anyway. Behind it all there was not, as might have been expected, some maharishi from distant India – the brain was American, from Texas. Some ten-gallon-hatted Texan cowboy whom they all called just Tex . . . Hesseltine suspected that investigation of Tex would reveal a history of mental instability, or perhaps he had just recognised a good racket. In brief – again according to little fat Annie – the commune hippies were ready for death. Literally.

"How literally?" Shard asked.

"Very. I gather there's no date fixed, but at some time in the fairly near future they're all to die. They can't wait. Once dead, they're to be airlifted by a UFO to await reincarnation in a better world, a hippie world presided over by a hippie God, all drugs and sex and lying about in the sun. A world where they'll all be hippies with no fuzz to offer harassment."

Shard said, "You did say they were bonkers, sir."

"That's right. All the same – if I may suggest this, Hedge – I believe they're worth investigating."

Hedge sniffed. " Up your street, no doubt."

"Not mine. Extra territorial."

"Interpol – "

"No." The ACC was firm. "Not them either. No crime is being committed – so far, anyway. I gather there *is* a financial angle insofar as those who have any money or possessions are to sign them over to Tex before the death date, but little fat Annie says nothing's been made over yet – "

"*Have* they any possessions?" Hedge asked sourly. "I thought hippies just stood about in their own stench."

Hesseltine said, "Mainly they do, of course. But quite a lot are from good families as we all know, and some of those families listen to appeals for money and cough up – stupid, but there it is. Parental guilt feelings, perhaps. Anyway, to get back to my suggestion: there's an obvious link with Asipov through the son, and that has become known via the commune." He got to his feet, glancing at his watch. "I'll leave you with the thought, Hedge. It'd broaden your mind, to join a hippie commune."

Hedge looked murderous. When Hesseltine had gone, Shard said, "He has a point, you know."

"Yes," Hedge snapped. "A ridiculous one. Damn it all, Shard, affairs of state aren't to be decided by persons called, what was it, little fat Annie!"

"Come off it, Hedge. Don't be so pompous. You know as well as I do, information can come from all sorts of unlikely sources. If Asipov's interrogation gets us nowhere, then I reckon little fat Annie might prove quite interesting. And don't forget – we haven't got all that long. When the time runs out, we may have to hand Asipov back. That won't be in *our* hands to decide."

Hedge glowered. "Are you suggesting you should go across to this wretched commune?"

"That's right, I am."

"Then the answer's no. I still haven't made up my mind about the Foreign Secretary's protection. In any case, your idea – it's nothing but a wild-goose chase, Shard. I feel convinced Asipov will talk once he's properly interrogated. Really, that's all we're concerned with. I'm not in the least concerned with Mrs whatsername and her past indiscretions –

26

or with her son. Frankly, I think Hesseltine's been wasting his time and mine. It's so like the Yard. They think as policemen. We're above that in the Foreign Office as you'd do well to remember, Shard."

"Sometimes," Shard said heavily, "I think we're so far above ordinary mortals – or you are, Hedge – that we don't see what's under our feet. If Asipov doesn't come up with anything within the next few hours, I'm bloody well going to visit that commune and you can stuff your orders up your jumper!"

Hedge sat speechless. Shard banged out of the room; Hedge shook with rage. Policemen were impossible; so common, so loud. Trenchard had had the right idea back before the war, in the thirties. Create an officer class, send them to a police college and turn out gentleman inspectors, with the hoi polloi confined to the lower ranks. Hedge thought purple thoughts about bribery and corruption and planted evidence, all the things that gentlemen never did. And damn Shard. Hedge was totally unprepared for disaster when the call came through from a very high place, so high that he automatically sat to attention as he listened, jaw sagging. There had been a raid on the Westminster Hospital, an armed raid. Never had there been anything like it. Guns in the wards, the nurses having hysterics . . .

The two FO interrogation experts were dead; so were the four plain clothes security officers. So was Stanislav Asipov, who would never talk now. The gunmen, dressed apparently as doctors complete with white coats and dangling stethoscopes, had simply walked in and no-one had challenged them. They had opened fire, a real execution squad with silencers fitted to the guns, and had then walked out again, as calmly as they had walked in.

It didn't sound like an Embassy job, though with the Russians you could never be sure. And it had been the Prime Minister on the line, in person – most unusual! That boded no good at all. No-one's job was safe these days when a balls-up happened and a redundant Hedge would obviously find a restricted labour market . . . His earlier thoughts about the police now submerged in the onset of panic, Hedge seized his internal line and shouted urgently for Shard.

3

All kinds of police had attended, naturally: fingerprints, forensic, diplomatic protection, homicide . . . but there were no leads at all. The officers who might have used their observation to better effect than the medics were all dead, and the rest of it had been panic. No faces memorised in any useful detail, hardly enough to make up an identikit caricature. In any hospital, men in white coats are never questioned and the getaway had been perfect. Not so much as a car number had been taken. As might have been expected, the Russian Embassy denied all knowledge; and the official feeling was that they had told the simple truth. Diplomats don't go in for such blunt methods.

What stood out was that someone had a good reason for the killing. Both the someone and the reason had to be found. And in the meantime the Russian Embassy was making trouble: the British were not going to get away with it. To allow such a thing to happen to an accredited trade delegate from Moscow was sheerly criminal. In fact, the tone of the Embassy's communications suggested beyond doubt that they believed the British to have been responsible, sending in their strong-arm men to do their dirty work for them. That way was easier than holding onto a Russian subject in face of Soviet opposition.

Hedge was still beside himself. "It probably has to do with the man who telephoned," he said to Shard. "If he rings again . . . but he probably won't."

"Doubtful, Hedge. That time limit he spoke of doesn't matter any more now."

"If only we knew *why* Asipov was killed!"

"Obviously, before he talked – "

"Yes, yes, Shard, but what about? That's what we have to

find out, isn't it?" Hedge almost collapsed into the swivel chair behind his desk. "God alone knows how. You'll have to dig hard."

Shard nodded. "In the absence of anything else, there's still little fat Annie."

"Those damn hippies!"

"All we've got," Shard said briefly. "We do know little fat Annie was in contact with the son in Moscow – Asipov's son as it turns out – "

"The non-person, Shard. What use is a non-person likely to be?"

"I don't know. Possibly none. But I repeat, it's all we have. We have to plug it. What's the Head's view?"

"I've not had a chance to talk to him about that yet," Hedge said irritably.

"In that case, I suggest you do it now."

*　　*　　*

That night Hedge went home very late and in a foul mood. The Head of Security had been fool enough to see it Shard's way; the hippie commune had to be investigated. He suggested an infiltration rather than what might be called a frontal assault. The hippies wouldn't be likely to respond to the long arm of the Foreign Office, seeing in that a threat to their happy existence, and in any case they were apparently not all British. Little fat Annie, H of S said, sounded interesting, a comment received by Hedge in affronted silence since it repeated what Shard himself had said earlier.

Hedge argued, but the orders were issued: Shard was to go to France and see what he could pick up and he was to be quick about it and get results before the diplomatic storm widened into a hurricane.

"And the Foreign Secretary's visit to Paris?" Hedge asked.

"What about Shard's DI?"

"Sick list," Hedge said. "A long business." He gave H of S the details, adding that there was no-one else available. H of S stared back at him, a glimmer of something like humour in his eye. They could, he said, always ask the Yard. Hesseltine

29

might fix someone from the Diplomatic Protection Squad. Hedge, furious at any suggestion that Hesseltine might be asked a favour, stepped right into it. He said, "They'll be there anyway. We need one of our own men . . . seeing it's the Foreign Secretary – "

"Yes, you're quite right, of course. As a matter of fact I'd like you to go, Hedge."

"Me?" Hedge sat bolt upright, shaken to the core.

H of S smiled. "Not exactly as a personal guard. I don't mean that. To be in overall charge, and very much under cover. Just keep handy really, that's all – as much to maintain contact with Shard as with the Foreign Secretary. I'm sure you'll enjoy it, though Paris in August does tend to be a shade hot . . ."

Back at his home in Chelsea, Hedge thumped angrily into bed. He had a headache and he didn't sleep at all well. In the morning he felt terrible and was faced with a very early start: H of S had wanted him to be in Paris well in advance of the Foreign Secretary's arrival, which would be by air from Heathrow the day after. In the interest of security Hedge was to leave England as a tourist, travelling by sea from Newhaven to Dieppe, a perfectly ghastly performance in Hedge's view, and he was to catch the ferry leaving Newhaven at 1000 hours. That meant leaving for Victoria at some frightful hour which, when Hedge glared sleeplessly at his watch, was almost upon him.

Vengefully, he heaved himself out of bed.

*   *   *

Shard had not gone home at all: there was much to do. He rang Beth and said casually that he'd be away for a few days and she wasn't to worry. He knew that, wife-like, she would; Beth was the world's worst worrier, but she knew better than to ask questions about duty. Shard sent a kiss down the line and turned his mind to work. He was to be accompanied to France by WDC Brett. Eve Brett . . . she'd done undercover work with him before and he knew her to be thoroughly reliable. Good cover, two hippies, a man and a girl, and he would enjoy her company.

During the night Shard and WDC Brett turned themselves into hippies. Physically it wasn't difficult: dirt was the main ingredient, the rest being jeans, T-shirts, beads and bangles, and some hair dye, plus sandals. Each of them was equipped with a handbag that dangled from a leather strap and a radio for blaring out along the street. False passports had been provided by the experts: names, Simon Shelley, occupation writer – he was too mature to pass as a student – and Eve Breedon, art student. The personal possessions each would take would be minimal.

"The test, the first test," Shard said with a dead-pan expression, "will come early."

"How's that, sir?"

He wagged a finger at her. "Sir's out from now, right?"

"Right," she answered. "And the test?"

"We're catching the same ferry as Hedge."

She gave an involuntary giggle. "Does he know?"

"He does not. I've just made the decision."

"Risky, surely?"

He shook his head. "No." Hippies didn't use airline tickets in any case, so it had to be a ferry, followed by a series of hitches. "If we survive Hedge we'll survive anything – not that he'll approach closely. We're too dirty, or soon will be. Fancy a ring through your nose, Eve?"

She shuddered. "No, thanks!"

"I'll spare you that, then."

They left as soon as they were ready. The transformation had been made, not at the FO security section, but at Shard's cover establishment in Seddon's Way off the Charing Cross Road where ostensibly he operated as a commercial philatelist, a handy job for making all kinds of underground contacts who hadn't to know his connection with the Foreign Office. The trip to France had to look authentic all the way, so he intended to start as he meant to go on, and that meant a hitch to Newhaven. They went down the stairs and out into dark streets, night-silent of traffic with patches of light coming from the strip joints and massage parlours. The odd prostitute drifted, defying the law but watching out for fuzz. Shard wished them the best of luck: the law was so often an ass. The prozzies performed a useful public service and if they'd been allowed to make themselves more obvious and available the sex-crime rate could have been cut by half. And there were better things for policemen to do than harass the women of the streets and prevent men getting what nature urged them to seek. Britain was fuller of dottiness every year . . . With Eve Brett, Shard started on the long drag out of London, making in the general direction of the M23 for Brighton. Luck was with them: they had just reached the Vauxhall Bridge Road with Shard's thumb stuck out like a flag when an artic stopped at some lights.

Shard approached the cab, looked in at the beefy-faced man with a mop of black hair that gave him a troll-like appearance. "Where for, mate?"

"Lewes."

"Great. Take us, will you?"

The troll said, "Sure, hop in."

They got aboard just as the lights changed. The artic pulled away. The troll didn't stop talking after asking where they were going. He said they would easily find a lift down from Lewes to Newhaven. France, he said, great place. Pity they weren't going to Paris: the Place Pigalle had all a man could want, so long as he didn't have his bird with him, he said with a grin at WDC Brett. Women, cor! Food was crap, not enough chips. But – once again – women, cor. He'd had a holiday there once, with the missus which took the shine off, but he'd been back since on long haul continental road transporters and it had been great. And yes, he knew the Ardeech. Heard about the hippie commune, too. What a lark. Pretty dirty by all accounts, piss where you stood, and then there were the entertainments. "All of them, having a f – know what I mean – all in the open. Not many of 'em bother to dress at all, not when the weather's right. Just like Stonehenge in July." He cleared his throat noisily and spat from the cab window. "Well, kiss my arse, good luck to the buggers."

They were quite sorry to part company with the troll-like man at Lewes, or more precisely just outside where the

32

artic stopped at a drivers' café. It was early yet, but the café was open. Shard had half an eye on breakfast, but a lorry was about to pull out for Newhaven so he took the offered opportunity.

★   ★   ★

It was not going to be a good crossing; Hedge took care to remain in the open air. He sat on a hard wooden bench, glowering at grey water as the ferry came past the end of the breakwater and out towards the open sea. There was already a nasty motion and he could only hope the seasick pills would prove effective. He made a dismal-looking tourist, not happy with his travelling companions, of which many were children and French at that. School parties. The ferry was French too, and appallingly dirty. The children were very badly behaved, racing dangerously about, quite out of control and making a lot of noise. Two of them sat for a while on Hedge's bench, giggling and making sotto voce remarks about him. Hedge closed his eyes and pretended not to hear. In fact it was unlike French children to make nuisances of themselves, French school discipline was very much better than was to be found in England, where there was none at all. Perhaps, he thought, they were having a last fling or had simply been led into bad ways by contact with the English.

Hedge simmered. When the children ran off, shrieking and yelling, they were replaced by a young couple who, once seated, immediately intertwined themselves just as though they were already in bed. Hedge left them to it and staggered up and down the open deck until he came across another bench, empty, which gave him more privacy. He thumped himself down gloomily. He was furious still at having been sent into the field. He was too senior, it was infra dig. It was all Shard's fault; if Shard hadn't gone on about that ridiculous woman in the hippie commune . . . and all the time he was away trouble was going to be piling up in Whitehall, trouble over dead Asipov. Hedge racked his brains: where, oh where, did Stanislav Asipov fit into the scheme of things? He simply had to have some sort of significance, and there was certainly

33

a possibility that he impinged in some way upon the Foreign Secretary's visit to Paris.

Hippies, Hedge thought angrily, there were all too many of them aboard the ferry. People who could be hippies, anyway: such curious clothing and an unwashed look, and many of them intertwined even in motion, like the stationary couple on the last bench. It was really disgusting. Two of them were leaning over a rail at the after end of the next deck up, looking down upon him. Filthy though they were, the man's hair wasn't as long as one expected of hippies and they were not intertwined, though close. They seemed to be enjoying a joke and Hedge had the feeling he was the cause of it. After a while they drifted away, and a change took place in Hedge's immediate neighbourhood: an elderly woman got up from the next bench and her place was taken by a middle-aged man wearing a check tweed jacket and dark grey trousers, very respectable-looking with a neat blue striped shirt and dark glasses. He opened a book. He had read no more than a page when a woman came past, looked down at him, and stopped.

"Why, Vicar, what a surprise!"

Confusion. The mufti-clad parson was caught off balance. "Well, well, Mrs Marks. It's you, fancy that."

"I was just saying to my husband, I *thought* it was you – how lucky. I wanted a word about the harvest festival . . ."

Hedge was virtuously pleased. It served the parson right, an excellent reminder that even when you embarked on a dirty week-end in Paris the eyes of the parish were upon you. The Church was as bad as anything else today.

*   *   *

There had been no contact between Hedge and Shard, but from the deck above Shard had caught Hedge's eye. He had seen no hint of recognition.

"Test passed," he said to Eve Brett, grinning. "How about a drink?"

They went to the bar, even there suffering the children like Hedge. In Dieppe they shuffled past the immigration control and customs; they could see Hedge ahead of them, saw him go aboard the Paris train standing in the dock siding. They went across the railway lines to the street, had rolls and coffee, expensively, in a café. The smell of France enfolded them, an aroma made up of drains or the lack of them, coffee, heat striking from the pavements, and, here in Dieppe, the smell of turgid water and oil fuel. They had a long haul ahead of them, right down to the Ardèche and the valley of the Rhône. The hippie commune was between the towns of Bourg St Andéol and Orange, around five hundred miles south-east from Dieppe. But once again luck was with them: leaving the café they went down past the docks towards the main railway station of the town and found a Dormobile with a British registration and a flat tyre. A young man and a girl were staring at it helplessly; inside the vehicle a baby screamed blue murder.

"Want a hand?" Shard asked. They were very grateful. Shard changed the wheel; conversation elicited the fact that the couple were making for Clermont Ferrand, very nicely on the way. There was no difficulty about a lift. That night they slept, deep in the French countryside, and by lunch time next day Shard and Eve Brett had been off-loaded in Clermont Ferrand and were looking for transport on the next leg south.

★   ★   ★

Hedge had found the Paris train quite excellent compared with British Rail: it was clean, there were little receptacles in which to place rubbish, it was air conditioned and it ran dead on time. The refreshment car gave excellent service and the doors between coaches actually worked, closing automatically as they were meant to, without fuss and heave. On the dot the train pulled smoothly into the Gare St Lazare and Hedge puffed along importantly to find a taxi. That was not so good; his taxi contained a ferocious-looking Alsatian that occupied the front seat next to its master, and hung its head in possibly friendly fashion over the back of the seat, mouth open, tongue lolling close to a frightened Hedge, the lips drooling rabies germs down onto his knees. When he edged away, the mouth followed. One nip and that might be the end of him. The drive was a nightmare of dog and traffic. The near misses were too

35

many to be counted, as were the oaths and shaken fists. Paris traffic worsened each year, Hedge thought frantically as the taxi fought its way through a roundabout and whizzed violently across the Place de la Concorde where, many years earlier, the crazy French had guillotined their aristocracy. If they'd had cars in those days, they might have been saved the trouble.

Hedge was bound for the Hotel Aviatic in the Rue de Vaugirard, and this destination had caused the taxi driver some heart searching: the Rue de Vaugirard was long and was one way. It would be hit or miss, an apt enough phrase on the Paris streets, and it turned out to be a miss. The driver made contact with the Rue de Vaugirard at the wrong point and Hedge had to disembark or face a long detour at the end of which there was no guarantee of success. The hotel, the driver said, was not far to walk.

"Scandalous," Hedge said in approximate French. The driver made a rude gesture and demanded twenty-five francs. Conscious of being diddled as an English tourist, Hedge added no tip and was hastened on his way along the Rue de Vaugirard by a stream of abuse. The Alsatian, wretched dog, barked at him. The walk was a very long one and Hedge had his bag to carry. He arrived at the Hotel Aviatic in a foul temper and wet through with sweat. Having checked in, he was taken up to his room on the fifth floor, and found it clean and comfortable; that cheered him. From his bag he brought a flask of whisky, then rang down for Vichy water, not trusting French taps – water in France was always suspect and at the very least led to diarrhoea if not dysentery. Room service was speedy and the girl was polite. Hedge poured and drank, felt better, unpacked and examined some tourist leaflets that he had picked up at the reception desk, since he was ostensibly a tourist . . . One of the attractions leapt to the eye immediately: starting after dark, a coach would leave on a Sex Tour of the Place Pigalle and other nefarious places. The price was approximately thirty pounds sterling plus extras, unspecified. Hedge muttered to himself: the French were, of course, sex mad and thought the English were the same.

36

He went down in the lift and left the hotel to make a telephone call. It was his duty to check in with the British Embassy. When at last he found a telephone and was answered, he was put through to the First Secretary. The First Secretary was easy and urbane, but Hedge detected an undercurrent. Perhaps Hedge, the First Secretary suggested, would find it convenient to come along to the Embassy?

★   ★   ★

Shard had found another lift, this time in a clapped-out truck full of chickens going to Bourg St Andéol. With WDC Brett he clambered aboard, squeezing into the cab with a mountainous Frenchwoman who thereafter drove as though she was demented, spending a good deal of the time with her body turned almost fully round to the back so she could watch the chickens, which were not in cages but bouncing about freely beneath a sort of criss-cross spider's-web of decrepit netting stretched over the open body of the truck. Every now and again she slammed a heavy foot on the brakes as a hen was disgorged onto the road in a squawking heap of disordered feathers. Each hen took some while to recover; Shard and Eve Brett helped in the operation, a messy one. As a result of this, despite the truck's lunatic speed, their arrival in Bourg St Andéol was late. In the town they asked the way to the hippie commune and were met by indrawn breaths and a lot of voluble comment. No decent person went near the commune, there were such goings on as could not be mentioned in polite conversation. They would have to walk; it was not many miles to the south, down in the Rhône valley. They would probably see a blaze of light, unholy light from flares and lanterns, and hear song and musical instruments, guitars mostly.

They set out. By this time they looked fully authentic and smelled it too. When at last they saw the promised light ahead, below them in the valley's depths, not far now, and heard the racket, they were still to some extent covered in chickens' feathers more or less glued to their clothes and bodies with chicken excrement; being hurtled to the ground at speed had been bad for the fowls' nerves.

The noise increased as they came closer. The guitars strummed. Naked bodies cavorted beneath a bright flare, and onlookers made loud comments and there was laughter. There was a gateway into the field, which was a large one, and the gateway was guarded by a skinhead clad in leather with many badges and other adornments including what looked like chain mail from the days of the Crusades, and carrying an iron spike with a ball at its end, the ball itself being covered with smaller spikes.

This person, chewing gum, barred their way.

He said, "Fuck off."

"Place is big enough," Shard said. "And free."

"Full house, man. Full house."

"We've come a long way."

"Go a long way back, then."

"All the way to England? Not us, man. We've come to join you . . . come to join Tex – "

"Tex, eh?" The skinhead stared back at them, chewing, hands on hips, spike dangling. "Tex. You converted?"

"Converted, man, yes. So let us in." Shard pushed forward. The skinhead took a pace backwards and lifted the spike, held the ball in Shard's face.

"Not so fast, not so fast. What's your names?"

"Simon and Eve."

"Eve, that's good. You want to come in, you wait here." The skinhead put a couple of fingers in his mouth and blew a blast, a loud, piercing whistle. From the circle of light a fat body emerged, a cigarette dangling from thick lips. There was a smell of pot. The face was bearded but not thickly, and behind the hair pimples showed, large and pink in the light from the flares. More hair sprouted from the armholes of a filthy, tattered vest. This man said, "Yeah?"

"Go get Tom Tit."

"Right." The man coughed, spat and turned away. The skinhead stayed silent, swinging his spiked ball, staring at the two visitors. Beneath the light, the entertainment continued to the accompaniment of the guitars. Somewhere in the distance a voice sang; Shard couldn't make out the tune or the words.

Naked bodies passed, uncuriously. The night was warm and dry; Shard wondered what it was like when it rained and turned the field to mud, the bodies to goose-pimples with wet hair. There was a weird feeling in the air, a feeling of unknown menace, almost primaeval, almost satanic. Those ridiculous UFOs . . . were all these people really waiting to embark, waiting for death to set them free of the twentieth century, fornicating their time away meanwhile? It was, he supposed, a belief of a sort and obviously a congenial one.

They had a long wait; they sat down on the grass verge of the road, outside the gate into the field. The iron spike and ball went on swinging, reflecting the light. From somewhere came a long-drawn scream, a woman's scream . . . Shard's basic police instincts came to the surface. It sounded like murder; here in the commune, rape would hardly raise such a scream. Rape would be no more than passing the time. He controlled his instincts; he had a job to do and his official rank would get short shrift here.

Tom Tit arrived at last. He was a blatant gay, swinging narrow hips, clad only in a vest and bother boots, a strange sight. A gay but a dangerous one, with a vicious narrow face and a slit for a mouth. Cheeks sunken as though he had no teeth . . . he was an oldie, all of fifty Shard believed, but he appeared to carry authority.

"What is it, Frigger?"

The skinhead swung his spike towards Shard and Eve. "These. Want in. Says they're converted, the feller does."

Tom Tit moved up closer. He stank like a sewer. He looked the two of them up and down, eyes narrowed. "Away from here," he said, "what do you do? Or did do, before you dropped out?"

Shard quoted their passports. "My girl's a student – was. Art student. I'm a writer. Ran out of inspiration. Or lost interest. It's all phoney, second-hand. I can't take any more."

Tom Tit asked, "You want to take a trip? I mean up there." He waved a hand towards the dark sky dappled with stars.

"That's right," Shard said. "There's peace, up there. No more hassle, right?"

39

"Right," Tom Tit said. "You could have to wait, duckie. There's a long list. Could even be years. Another thing: you'll be put through a test. That okay?"

"Yes," Shard said, not knowing to what ordeals he might be committing Eve Brett. He took a deep breath. "Look," he said to Tom Tit, "who're you in the set-up? I've heard about Tex, but – "

Tom Tit broke in sharply. "Tex, he's the Saviour, see, man? I'm number two . . . like I'm Jesus Christ's mate. You'll see Tex later. Come inside."

They went in. Tom Tit minced with them through the crowd, side-stepping the bodies, some of whom were asleep. There seemed to be no shelter anywhere, and once again Shard wondered about inclement weather. Perhaps that was part of the purgatory that pointed up the paradise parts. And when the UFOs took off at some time in the future, there would be no more rain, no more tears. They went with Tom Tit to the far side of the field towards a line of trees beyond. Between the field and the trees was a hedge. "Get down and sleep," Tom Tit said. He left them, after saying there would be a meal in the morning, early. The hippies were early risers, he said. Before breakfast there would be prayers, and they would see Tex.

As the gay minced off, Eve said uneasily, "I don't see any likely connection between this place and Asipov. Do you?"

"Not at the moment. It's early days."

"Yes, but . . . how do we contact little fat Annie?"

Shard grinned at her in the darkness. "We don't rush it, for a start. We just keep our eyes skinned for a girl who's little, and fat, and whose name is Annie. Right? I don't think we'll have all that much trouble identifying her, somehow."

Dead tired as they were, neither of them slept much that night. There was too much noise, for one thing, that went on until the early hours with the dawn not far off – the hippies must have iron constitutions. And Shard was only too well aware that time might be short, an awareness that inhibited relaxation. Back in London, urgency had surrounded Asipov. And next day the Foreign Secretary was due to arrive in Paris.

4

The First Secretary's name was Roberts-White and he was well known to Hedge. Hedge was equally well known to Roberts-White, who could have done without his presence in Paris at a busy and difficult time; but crosses had to be borne with diplomatic equanimity and Roberts-White was politeness itself as he welcomed Hedge to his office in the Embassy.

"Delighted," he said. "Nice to see you again."

Hedge grunted; there had been something not far off a mob in the Rue du Faubourg St Honoré and he had arrived breathless and a shade distraught. "What's all that in aid of?" he asked, jerking a hand towards the windows. "Blasted French . . ."

Roberts-White gave a cough. "Yes, well. Oh, it's nothing much – "

"Blasted Latin temperament, I suppose. But it must have a purpose, surely?"

"Certain sections," Roberts-White said smoothly, "are against the Foreign Secretary's visit. HE's not too worried, but of course we do face problems of security as you'll be well aware, naturally."

"It's what I'm here for. And I suppose that's what you wanted to talk to me about." Hedge added with a touch of plaintiveness, "I've not eaten yet, you know. Dinner."

"Yes, quite. Same here. Unfortunately I can't get home – you'll understand, I'm sure – or I'd have suggested you dine with us." The First Secretary told a glaring white lie on his wife's behalf. "Elizabeth will be disappointed not to see you, Hedge."

"Nice of her," Hedge said. "And I her." This was true;

Elizabeth Roberts-White was an honourable, the younger daughter of a viscount no less, and the snob in Hedge was always well to the fore. Roberts-White went on to say that he would arrange for a meal to be sent up, to be taken while they discussed the security arrangements, managing to make it discreetly clear that he meant he would fill Hedge in on what had already been decided. Hedge was to be the gingerbread-work, the gilt that had to be accorded a VIP such as the Foreign Secretary. Hedge could read between the lines. His field was to be no more than a ceremonial lawn.

Nevertheless he had a feeling, a nasty feeling, that he had not been brought to the Embassy just to hear this. And he was right. The preliminaries over, the First Secretary got down to the nitty gritty.

"There's just one other thing," he said. He turned as a discreet knock came at the door. A little earlier he had pressed a button in a box on his desk and spoken briefly into it; and now a servitor had appeared with menu cards, one of which was handed to Hedge. "Just a little something," Roberts-White murmured. "The *daube de boeuf à la provençale*'s rather good usually." They settled for that, after prawns with cream, brandy sauce and rice, and Roberts-White ordered a bottle of Gevrey-Chambertin to go with the *boeuf*. When the servant had withdrawn he went on with what he had been about to say earlier. "Just one thing."

"Yes?"

"Stanislav Asipov," Roberts-White said.

Hedge stiffened. "What about him?"

"We've just had word through from the FO. It's believed he was a plant."

"I'd half suspected that," Hedge lied.

Roberts-White raised an eyebrow. "Had you? Well done!"

Hedge flushed. Tartly he said, "Tell me about it. How's it emerged he was a plant?"

"It hasn't emerged exactly. It's what Whitehall now thinks. The fuss from the Russians has a synthetic ring, apparently. There's no value to us in Asipov, he's just what he always was on the surface, a technical expert in his own field, which is – "

"Gas pipelines."

"Yes. Nothing very earth-shaking, expect perhaps in a purely physical sense – "

"What? Oh – yes, I follow. Very droll. But if he was a plant, what was he being planted *for*? Simply as a long term spy?"

Roberts-White nodded. "Spot on, Hedge." He paused, then went on, "It's being suggested that someone was precipitate in having Asipov hooked off that Russian jet. We reacted just as the Russians expected we would, after they'd rigged that dash from the factory and then given chase – "

Savagely Hedge said, "He's dead now in any case."

"Yes. We still don't know, I gather, who that telephone call came from, the one that said he'd be dead in a couple of days if – "

"I took the call myself," Hedge snapped, "so I'm fully aware of what was said."

"But I'm told," Roberts-White went on in disregard of the interruption, "that some progress has been made in another direction. The gunmen slipped up. Early this morning a stethoscope was found in the Westminster Hospital . . . that's to say it was actually found *yesterday* in a corner by the main entrance and handed in to the porters' office. At the time, no-one ticked over. Then it was realised – when no-one claimed the stethoscope – that the Yard might be interested – "

"Because the gunmen had gone in disguised as doctors?" Hedge asked keenly.

"Quite. So it was collected and sent down to the fingerprint people. After the eliminations, one set stood out. This was checked with the computer and identified."

"Someone with a criminal record?"

Roberts-White nodded. "Internationally. A Russian dissident by the name of Alexander Vernodski. Heard of him, Hedge?"

"No."

Roberts-White looked surprised. "Well, he's known here in Paris. He's a member of a group dedicated to the overthrow of the Soviets, a pretty hopeless task if you ask me, but there you are, they're fanatics. No doubt you know of them – "

43

"Possibly." Memories of days past . . . Hedge asked, "Are you referring to the Avengers of St Petersburg?"

"Yes, I am – "

"And the connection with Asipov?"

"Vernodski was Asipov's half brother."

"Yet he killed Asipov?" Hedge's mind was in a whirl and he was remembering Ernestine Kolnisenko and her bastard son Mikhail – Vernodski's nephew, evidently. Hedge mopped at his face. "Why kill his own brother?"

"We don't know whose hand fired that particular shot," Roberts-White pointed out. "As a member of the Avengers of St Petersburg he was probably simply following orders, or even demonstrating his commitment. Also, brotherly love is not a universal thing by any means. And he was only a half brother, remember."

Hedge's brain whirled still. It was all too much for him and he was feeling his age; he should be back in London . . . it was all happening in his absence and it was never a help to anyone's career to be seen to be dispensable. Dabbing again at his face he asked, "These Avenger people . . . you said Vernodski's known in Paris. Is he here now, do you suppose?"

"Unlikely, Hedge. UK has had all ports and airports under close watch – you'll know that, of course – and the French are watching all entry points just as closely."

Hedge wrung his hands. "That's all very well, but his involvement wasn't known until – "

"Vernodski's always being watched for."

"Then how did he get out in the first place?"

Roberts-White shrugged. "He could have been many months in the UK, Hedge. Though certainly I'd have expected the Home Office and your people to know. There seems to have been a balls-up if you ask me."

The "little something" was brought in soon after but Hedge failed to do it justice; his appetite had gone. The expression balls-up was a disgusting one for a diplomat to use but there was no denying it fitted and it could well, in the course of time, be crammed down in an even tighter fit over his, Hedge's, ears. Of course it was Shard again; Shard should

44

have kept him informed about this Alexander Vernodski, he'd been guilty of the most enormous, the most flagrant, dereliction of duty. Names flashed through Hedge's brain as he picked at the *boeuf à la provençale:* Stanislav Asipov, Ernestine and Mikhail Kolnisenko, adultery and unexpected relationships that seemed about to impinge on international relations themselves . . . Alexander Vernodski who might be, was in fact, some kind of link.

What link, for God's sake? Was the Foreign Secretary – was that important personage in extra danger?

Roberts-White, reassuringly, didn't think so. He made some vague reference to the fact that in any case the security was exceptionally strong and Hedge himself was there too. Hedge didn't like the 'too': he considered he was an integral part of the strength already referred to. Roberts-White said there was nothing to worry about – not until he got back to London. There was no immediacy about the Asipov/Vernodski tangle and he had been informed only as a matter of courtesy and routine.

Was there just a hint that he wasn't being regarded as seriously as was his due? Another worrying thought: had H of S sent him to Paris just to get rid of him?

Hedge left the Embassy in a very bad temper and filled with morbid thoughts. He was under orders to stay in Paris so he couldn't very well go back to London until the Foreign Secretary did. Not unless he contacted H of S by the closed line from the Embassy and this he had already rejected, since all he could say in effect was that he was bloody useless in Paris and they could get on well enough without him. Walking along the Rue du Faubourg St Honoré – the mobs had gone now – Hedge found himself in a curiously bitter and defeated mood. Everything nagged at him; Shard was a beastly nuisance, getting himself sent to that dreadful hippie commune in the south of France. Hedge's inflamed imagination blossomed and ran riot, ran the full gamut of all that he knew, or guessed, went on in hippie communes. God alone could say what Shard might be getting up to, even if only in the interest of authenticity in his role. Open-air copulation, sex of all kinds beneath the moon, beneath the sun as well, the hippies didn't let that inhibit them. Interesting, perhaps, to play the voyeur . . .

Voyeur?

That brochure . . . Hedge looked almost guiltily at his watch. It was far from late, far from too late if he hurried.

But no, he couldn't possibly! It wasn't to be thought of for one second. A pillar of the Foreign Office, ranking with an assistant under-secretary of state! One who moved in exalted circles, mixed with ministers of the crown, smiled at on one occasion by the Queen herself. It would be unforgivable, of course it would. But life was hard and this was Paris and Hedge had suffered his frustrations for long enough. A widower these many years, and his wife had never been keen on it anyway . . . nature still called loud and clear and coursed strongly in his veins.

Hedge walked on, heart pumping, lewd scenes coming into his mind. He would *accompany* the tour, nothing more. But it was appalling . . . he went so far as, there in the Rue du Faubourg St Honoré, to plead with God to remove the scenes and their horrible temptations from his mind; but God failed to respond. He could still reach the assembly point, which – why he didn't know – he had memorised from the hotel pamphlet.

He would go.

Why not for goodness' sake? It wasn't a crime. Gay Paree – and he was here on his own. Other diplomats did it. All those reports from Moscow and Washington.

But he *couldn't* go. On the other hand . . . being watchful, conscientious, observing places where men with wicked intentions against the Establishments of East and West might foregather? Possibly it could be justified.

He did something stupid: he went. He made his way along the Paris streets to the assembly point for the coach party and upon arrival found a motley crowd already waiting, some sheepish, others blatant. Not all male: two butch girls had turned up and when the coach came they sat together in the rear, glaring at the back of the men's heads. Hedge's other companions were mostly middle-aged and mostly respectable, city and professional people who'd bypassed the wife for the evening. Some were young – four men in their early twenties come along for a giggle. Hedge felt contaminated but was determined to proceed even if he was the one who was to be giggled at. It was a man's duty, a diplomat's duty in particular, to broaden his mind and see how the basic people, the common people, lived and took their pleasures. It began to take on the air of an assignment almost. There would be no compulsion on him to take part in whatever turned up to be taken part in – none at all. He would be the amused onlooker, detached, one of the gigglers really, only in a more mature way. The young men were sitting across the aisle from him, as it happened, and he turned to them with a matey smile, but that didn't come off.

It was misunderstood; all he got was a glare and a loud remark about old poufs who should have taken a different sort of tour.

The coach started off. There was a girl acting as courier, which Hedge thought just showed how insensitive the blasted French were – either that or they were much too relaxed about sex. She was an attractive girl and her broken English was attractive too. She announced over a microphone that the sex part of the tour would not start immediately; there were other attractions in Paris, she said with a smile. "Ze English we treat with respect . . . sex is not all, zere is also Notre Dame."

They crossed the Seine to L'Ile de la Cité and looked at Notre Dame. They didn't go inside; perhaps that would have been disrespectful. They looked at the Pompidou Centre, all contorted with enormous pipes like a mad organ – why did *that* word have to come to mind, Hedge wondered – and they looked at a number of other places briefly, places that Hedge scarcely took note of. The blood pounded when they came at last into Montmartre and the Place Pigalle and he could hardly wait. He stared out of the coach window at the bright lights. Outlines of naked women, first one breast lit up then the other. Other suggestive things, adverts, neons, curious people lurking with curious desires no doubt. Disgusting, of course, but . . . to be honest Hedge had so far found nothing that was not part of the Soho scene but this was Paris and so the ambience was much more vital and soon they would be bound to see something really worth while.

The coach stopped and the courier ordered the sex tourers out into the street. She led them down a narrow and smelly alley and stopped at a door beneath the overhang of a balcony. There was music coming from above, a thud of drums and a wailing voice. The courier knocked three times, which Hedge knew was sheer propaganda, the sort of thing that made it all more mysterious and wicked, the thirty pounds more worth while.

A grille opened, more nonsense, and a nose was vaguely seen before they were admitted.

The stench was dreadful. Cheap scent, poor drains, foul lavatories, sweat. Hedge followed in a long queue, along a dark passage and then up some stairs where the drums hit with the force of all-out war.

They went into a small, jam-packed auditorium.

There was a stage. Such goings-on . . . Hedge clicked his tongue but was riveted all the same. A totally naked girl, almost immobile. Not quite . . . she was slowly, tantalisingly, bending her knees, lowering her body towards an object on the stage beneath her.

What was it? Hedge peered from tip-toe. A bottle – yes, an empty bottle of Johnny Walker complete with label.

Goodness gracious! Hedge was even more riveted. He had heard of this from people who'd visited Port Said and such places but he'd never really believed the stories. But there it was happening before his very eyes, and successfully too.

When the bottle was lifted, the courier ordered the party out again. There was no time to linger, there was much else to see, and later they would have some time on their own, or rather, apart from each other. There was an establishment well recommended by the tour organisers with comfortable dunlopillo mattresses. By this time Hedge was sweating like a pig and his head felt full of blood and no thought of Whitehall was entering his mind.

*   *   *

Soon after the dawn had stolen over the Ardèche the hippie encampment began stirring. Shard and Eve Brett, having dropped at last into an uneasy sleep, sat up in appreciation of fresh air and a golden mist hanging over the trees at the end of the field.

Eve said, "I'm hungry. Very."

"The man said, prayers first."

"Yes. Shorter the better. Who do we pray to, do you know?"

"No idea," Shard said. "Tex, probably, linked in with Tom Tit."

"You pray to ethereal beings, not physical ones."

"Well," he said, "we'll see soon." He was wondering how Hedge was making out. Somehow he couldn't see him in Paris. Eve got to her feet, stretching away the night's cramps. Her clothing felt damp, but dampness hadn't appeared to harm the hippies. There was movement going on now, a kind of straggly muster as the hippies gathered in groups under what looked like individual prayer leaders. From under a distant hedge a tall, rangy man emerged and strode through the assembling groups until he was more or less in the centre of them. He wore a long purple robe like a bishop's cassock and on his head was a western-style ten-gallon hat, an incredible sight, as reported earlier in London by Hesseltine.

"Tex," Shard said.

"Hi," a voice called. Shard turned. Tom Tit was approaching, waving a hand, gesticulating towards the group nearest to Shard and Eve. They took the hint and joined it; no-one appeared in the least curious about them; the hippies had somewhat dead expressions, withdrawn – until they caught the eye of Tex. Then looks of rapt adoration spread across the unwashed faces.

Tex, ten-gallon hat and all, revolved slowly in the centre,

beaming a smile, so far as Shard could make out, towards each group in turn. Shard, while this was going on, did a rough count: there must have been something like three hundred hippies in the field, a good if captive congregation. Then Tex lifted a hand, removed his hat with a show of reverence, presumably towards himself since he was God, and raised his arms in the air. As he did so all the hippies except for the prayer leaders went down on their knees. Shard and Eve did likewise. From their rear came a sonorous intonation. Shard glanced round. Tom Tit was uttering a prayer. "God who has left America and the warmongers and the moneymakers, those who would hold all persons in wage bondage and those who would enslave the free spirit of personkind, God who has rejected the imprisonment of the capitalist society to come to us here and lead us to the light, hail!"

"Hail," the prayer leaders repeated. Tex looked smug. More hails came from the kneeling hippies then in each of the groups a person, male or female, got up and flourished either a guitar or a banjo. Something like pandemonium broke out as each instrument went into a different tune. The hippies rose to their feet and leapt around to the music, shouting and in some cases screaming. The noise was indescribable. Shard and Eve gyrated with the rest; this was no doubt all part of morning prayers. Tex was seen to be swaying to the nearest rhythm, his eyes closed. Around him the hippies closed in to sway in unison, eyes closed like those of Tex, tears pouring down some of the cheeks, leaving runnels through the dirt. Some of them began to take off their clothes; in many cases this was an unedifying sight. Pot bellies indicated only a short time since the last meal of chips, and past burning of bras had left breast muscles in a sorry state.

Suddenly there was a yell from Tom Tit and the racket mercifully stopped dead. This was evidently Tex's cue. Once again the American lifted his hands in the air and went into a lengthy spiel. The gist of it was that the wait for the light would still be long but would be found well worth while; when the first of the UFOs came in to land, the time would be nigh and death would be the release. It would be all systems go and lift-off would take them straight to joy everlasting. In the meantime the kitty was always in need of cash and it would be better for the hippies' or if applicable their parents' souls if they parted with it, so Tex hoped that the message would go forth and be heeded.

When he had finished they all shouted, conventionally enough, Amen. That was the end of prayers; breakfast was next and all over the field primus stoves started up. There seemed to be a reasonable commissariat, each group produced its own from plastic bags ex supermarket – sausages, tomatoes, loaves of bread, even a tin of sardines in Shard's group. The hippies were generous; love was their watchword. They shared the food out. One, a young man as thin as a skeleton and with a pronounced limp – polio? – was very friendly.

"It's not fair to take yours," Shard said.

"It's yours too, man. It was put into the world for us all to share. Take it. You're old, man. You need it."

Shard, early thirties, younger he believed than Tex, took it and asked where it came from.

"Heaven," the hippie said. He seemed to mean it.

"Tex?"

"Right, man. Tex is the intermediary. He provides."

"And you don't question it?"

"No, man." Dark eyes, reproving eyes, were turned on Shard. "Nor do you."

"Sorry I spoke," Shard said, and took a torn-off hunk of bread. He and Eve got a sausage each plus a taste of fried tomato. Having found a friend of a sort, Shard took advantage of him. "Do you," he asked casually, "know a girl called little fat Annie?"

"Of course, man. Everybody knows little fat Annie. Little fat Annie's a disciple."

"Of Tex?"

"Right."

"How does a disciple rank, vis-à-vis the rest?"

Chewing, the hippie stared at Shard. He said, "You'll see, man, you'll see."

51

"Is she here now?"

"Yes, she's here. She's been away, but she's come back. You know her, man?"

"Friend of a friend," Shard said briefly. When breakfast was over the lame hippie kindly said he would take Shard to meet little fat Annie. That was, he would do so if she was not having intercourse with Tex, a frequent occurrence. The hippie went a little distance away to perform his toilet and when he came back he was talkative and Shard began to get the significance of the disciples. They were the ones, mainly female, whom Tex fancied and who had the honour, whether or not they had boy friends or girl friends of their own, of ministering – as the hippie put it – to their saviour Tex. Sex, the hippie said, was the mainspring of life and Tex was entitled to his tribute. Shard asked about death.

"That will come," the hippie told him seriously. "As soon as the UFOs are ready, like Tex said."

"And you're ready for it?"

"Yes, man, all ready."

He spoke with genuine assurance. He seemed to have no doubts at all that death was best and would lead to everlasting joy on Tex lines. Tex, Shard thought, must have something, but the others had to be, as Hesseltine had said back in London, crazy. As the groups dispersed for another day of lying about in the sun and playing the interminable guitars, the hippie kept his promise and took them across to a hummock of thickly-growing grass. On the far side of it was a very fat, placid-looking girl of about twenty; obviously little fat Annie, and not currently engaged with Tex or anyone else. She was sitting by herself, humming a tune, her large body swaying and her eyes closed. Shard thought he had never seen such a fat girl. The breasts were enormous, with a tremendous sideways spread, and were held in some sort of restraint by a very stained garment like a maternity dress gathered at the neck by a length of string. The material was thin enough to show the nipples pointed like protruding eyes at Shard and Eve Brett.

"Someone who knows you, Annie," the hippie said, and

limped off about his own business. Shard smiled down at the fat girl, who smiled back. She had a bovine look, one of being a shade simple. He said, "Hullo."

"English?"

"Yes."

She gave a pout; her face was broad and flat, Slav-looking. She said in a good but accented English, "You I do not know. Who are you, please?"

"The name's Simon."

"Ah, Simon."

"I know a friend of yours. Ernestine Kolnisenko."

"Yes."

"You went to see her in London."

"How do you know this?" There was, Shard thought, a hint of fear.

He squatted down beside her. "She told me – and you don't have to worry. I'm not here to harm you, Annie. Just want some information, that's all. About Mikhail Kolnisenko, who wants to contact his mother, the one you met."

"Mikhail?"

"Yes. You know him, don't you – in Russia?"

Candid eyes stared from rolls of flesh. She said, "Yes, I know him. Why do you want to know?"

"Because of his mother. She's worried, naturally. I'm told you brought news that he's a non-person, that though he's alive he's officially dead."

She nodded. "Yes. What do you want of me that I have not already told Mikhail's mother?"

"Nothing much. Nothing for you to be afraid of, Annie. Just tell me about him . . . how he manages to live, where he's living, whether he has any chance of getting out of Russia, perhaps to join his mother in England."

"That is all, you ask only because of his mother?"

Shard said, "I ask because I want to know, more precisely, why Mikhail wanted you to contact his mother, Annie. Can you tell me that?"

"It was a simple message," little fat Annie answered, shrugging. Shard didn't press; he asked instead if Mikhail or his

53

mother had ever mentioned a man called Asipov. "Stanislav Asipov. Think, Annie. It's important, or may be."

"Asipov," she repeated. "He was Mikhail's . . ." Her voice trailed away and Shard saw that she was no longer with him, no longer paying any attention. She was staring past him and Eve Brett and there was a weird expression on her face, a transformation, a spread of rapture, of devotion – of discipledom. Knowing who he would see, Shard turned. Tex.

Shard got to his feet, slowly, watching the American as he came closer. Tex looked down at little fat Annie. "Okay," he said softly. "You stay put for now. You two, move out ahead of me – and watch it."

Tex had brought a 9mm Stechkin APS from beneath the purple cassock.

5

Hedge had been suffering, both mentally and physically. He
had done appalling things, the more appalling to him now
because he had enjoyed them, by and large. It had been the
most incredible night of his life. His experiences in the course
of it had been totally different from what circumstances
had told him married life was like. Totally different and
very exhausting, and afterwards very worrying indeed. Of
course, the French women were said to be clean, they were
properly licensed, but terrible diseases could still lurk,
diseases that were unmentionable in Foreign Office circles and
certainly never to be caught by anyone in Whitehall – the
disgrace!

It had been three a.m. when Hedge had torn himself away
from the eager and expensive embrace of a young woman
of amazing energy and persistence and a good deal of what
Hedge considered invention. Much money had changed hands,
indeed Hedge was now penniless and would remain so until he
reached his hotel – and when he had emerged from the den of
sin the coach party had gone.

Oh dear, oh dear!

Where was he, where was the hotel?

He paused on the threshold of the establishment, trying
to collect his tormented wits. What the Head of Security
would say didn't bear thinking about, and as for the Foreign
Secretary . . . there were ways in which things could come out
and he could be blackmailed. And here he was, responsible –
up to a point – for the Foreign Secretary's safety whilst the
great man was in Paris. All Shard's fault.

Shaking in every limb and utterly lost, Hedge left the
brothel and set off along the filthy alley in which he had found

himself. It was dark, which didn't help, no street lights anywhere that he could see. Certainly no friendly policeman on the beat. And it was beginning to rain.

Hedge pattered along and he hadn't gone far when he heard the footsteps behind him. He didn't dare look round. A footpad after his non-existent cash – someone who might take his credit cards and by some nefarious process connect the name on them with Hedge of the Foreign Office, the feared blackmailer come true?

Oh, what a fool he'd been!

Never, never again. He put on speed; so did the footsteps. In a matter of moments they had overtaken him and a hand had reached out and grabbed his shoulder, swinging him round, close to an unshaven, threatening face.

"Let me go, you – you blackguard!" Hedge said in a high voice.

There was a grin and the teeth showed, very white in the fearsome darkness, the darkness where, in Paris, so much danger lurked. "No. I have long, long wait. I see you enter, and wait. I not let you go. I know who you are."

The accent, Hedge was convinced, was Russian. He shook with fear. He said with an attempt at dignified bravery, "Rubbish. You can't know who I am. I'm not important."

"You are Hedge," the man said, grinning again. "I know. I follow from your British Embassy . . . you board the coach of sex. I know where this goes, and I wait. Now you come with me."

"No! Leave me alone. I've never heard of anyone called Hedge, you've got the wrong man."

"No. I know. You are in Paris for your Foreign Minister. Come." The grip tightened on Hedge's shoulder. In utter panic now, Hedge reacted in a way that normally he would never have believed possible: he brought his knee up sharply and hurt the man where it hurt most. There was a gasp of pain, the grip fell away as the man doubled up, and Hedge was off down the alley as though the devil himself were behind him. He heard a phutting sound and a bullet sped past his left ear to smack into a building on a corner ahead. Hedge rushed on, heart thudding loudly and painfully, swerved round the corner, saw a nasty dark hole immediately in front of him, gave a whinney of terror and leapt clean over it. The man behind him was not so lucky: Hedge heard a yell, a smothered one, and the footsteps stopped. There was a crashing sound. Presumably the man had gone down into a cellar, the lid of which had been foolishly and dangerously left open.

No backward looks: Hedge ran on like the wind, puffing hard. Before long his heartbeats forced him to slow down: he could have a seizure if he wasn't careful, he wasn't as young as he was, and especially after such a night . . . but he still walked fast and, having done some twisting and turning after the man had gone down the hole, he felt he had got away with it. He should be safe in his hotel, at least during the daylight hours. No-one, supposing the man knew – which most probably he did – where he was staying, would attack in broad daylight. If only he wasn't lost; but all things come to an end and by six o'clock Hedge had picked up his bearings and people were beginning to appear on the streets. And then he had a stroke of luck: he found a fifty-franc note blowing along the street. It fetched up by a used contraceptive, but never mind. Finders keepers . . . Hedge picked it up. When he found a tobacconist's shop, he went in and bought a book of Metro tickets and went down into the nearest station. He got out at Saint-Placide and scuttled along the Rue de Vaugirard and took the risk of using the telephone to call the Embassy.

After some delay he got Roberts-White. The First Secretary sounded cold. He said, "Good heavens, I know it's early but I've been trying to get in touch. Where've you been?"

"Never mind that," Hedge snapped, going red at the telephone. "I must see you urgently, but I'm not coming to the Embassy." Instinctively he lowered his voice. "My life's been threatened. I've been *shot at*. When can we meet?"

"Soon as possible. Coq d'Or in the Champs Elysées – say in half an hour."

"That's – " Hedge pulled the receiver from his ear and glared at it angrily. Roberts-White had rung off, which was rude and impertinent. He, Hedge, took rank and precedence above First Secretaries. He went up in the lift to his room and called room service for a continental breakfast. Whilst doing this he noticed that his window was ajar, and he remembered positively closing it before leaving the evening before. Some careless servant . . . but then he saw that a pane had been broken.

Goodness gracious.

His things. And somebody, if there had been a somebody, had had a monumental job of cat burglary – fifth floor! Hedge quickly examined his things. He believed they had been gone through – they definitely had, his pants were not as he had so meticulously laid them in a drawer, and a shirt looked as though it had been disturbed. But his money was intact. No cash motive there. No doubt there was some connection with the man who had followed him; there might have been an accomplice. Now Hedge stood in more danger; attack could come from any quarter. But there was an amateurish quality about it all so far. The man outside the brothel – Hedge shuddered at the word – had seemed unprofessional in his approach, all those running footsteps, and then to plunge down a hole in the pavement! And the searcher of his things had been, to say the least, careless. A properly conducted search should never be so immediately obvious to the victim. They did things much better in the Foreign Office, but then of course they were British. Finally, to break a window was ludicrous, very ham-handed indeed.

Hedge, the professional, felt better about it.

He reached the Champs Elysées via the Metro from Saint-Placide, peering about for a tail. He didn't identify one, though he had a bad moment when a dreadful-looking, swarthy Frenchman who had boarded the same train as himself also got off at the Champs Elysées, but the man went off in a different direction. Hedge asked a woman where the Coq d'Or was. When he reached it – it was a pavement café – Roberts-White was there already with a cognac in front of him. He was reading some French newspaper; he glanced at Hedge over the top of it but gave no sign of recognition. He meant to be hole-in-corner; Hedge, no fool, took the hint but angrily. He had a lot to impart. He sat down and ordered café au lait. Roberts-White drank his cognac slowly. Hedge's order came; he had nearly finished the café au lait when Roberts-White got to his feet and sauntered away towards the Arc de Triomphe. Hedge gave him a start then got under way behind him. Roberts-White halted to look in a shop window. Hedge did likewise, feeling suddenly foolish. If anyone was watching he or she would know very well who they both were and the play-acting was superfluous. Roberts-White was being extra careful simply because he was dealing with Hedge, the security man from Whitehall in person. No feet would be put wrong. Commendable but a blasted nuisance. Hedge's irritation increased and he snapped, "Really, none of this is necessary, Roberts-White." The First Secretary seemed quite relieved. He said, "Oh, well, yes. I'm inclined to agree, but – "

"We shall walk," Hedge said, pompously. They did; they went on towards the Arc de Triomphe, pushing through bands of tourists, largely American. Ice-cream was everywhere, so were the purveyors of it, in stalls and mobile dispensaries, and the dusty so-called pavement was a mass of thrown-away paper and chewing-gum. The Champs Elysées had declined in elegance, like Princes Street in Edinburgh and the Burlington Arcade in London. So many common people about, the sort who in pre-war days would have kept to the back streets . . . what a bane trade unionism and tourism were. Hedge gave a bowdlerised account of his night's activities, skirting round the brothel rather quickly. Roberts-White didn't, luckily, prove inquisitive; but when Hedge came to the hole in the pavement he got a surprise.

Roberts-White said, "I know."

"You do? May one ask how?"

"By all means. Your man was found, having made quite a din in his descent. He was dead. Neck broken."

"The police – "

"Yes, they were called."

"But they didn't call you, I assume."

"Oh, no. You know how it is." Hedge did, of course; the

59

man clearly hadn't been British so the police wouldn't have connected, but the ears of diplomacy were long-range and, like spiders' webs, caught things. But Hedge was forced to ask, "Why did you connect it with *me*?"

"I didn't until just now – not all that many people fall down holes, you know. Another point: the man who did was special."

Hedge glanced sideways. "He's been identified, has he?"

"Yes. Alexander Vernodski – remember what I told you?"

Hedge did: Vernodski had been the half brother of Stanislav Asipov. Things were coming together, but how? Hedge said accusingly, "You assured me he wasn't in France, Roberts-White."

"No, I didn't. I did say it was unlikely . . . we're all human, you know. Slips can occur. It seems one has, but that's not my fault. Nor yours either," Roberts-White added magnanimously. "Blame the French police."

"These French," Hedge said witheringly. He pondered; they walked on, two British rocks in a sudden whirlpool eruption of French schoolchildren surging towards the Arc de Triomphe with three teachers presumably doing a holiday task on French martial glory. Hedge, fighting for breath as he was buffeted about, remembered, from a previous visit to Paris, walking from the Eiffel Tower to the French Military Academy and finding a great sign proclaiming that the latter was the home of the world's finest army, or words to that effect. Impertinent rubbish, he'd considered that – it had probably been instigated by de Gaulle and had lingered on. Anyway, the French had now been guilty of what Roberts-White would no doubt call a balls-up. Alexander Vernodski had meant trouble and should never have been allowed to worm his way into France. Hedge preened for a moment; *he* had dealt with that! The Foreign Secretary should be grateful, probably would be. Hedge asked, "Do you think there's a connection, Roberts-White?"

"With what?"

"Oh, the Foreign Secretary!" Hedge snapped. "His visit!"

"I'm beginning to think there might be. And there's something else. Word came through during the night. The PM's coming. The visit's been delayed three days on that account – you can imagine the hoo-ha. The French aren't pleased at all, all the preparations, you know. But Whitehall's adamant, for various reasons – "

"So now the Prime Minister's at risk!"

"I'm afraid it's possible. It's all rather a panic."

"Panic!" Hedge avoided an ice-cream cone, held aloft by a French child. "All we need now is the Queen . . . "

★   ★   ★

Hedge simmered gently beneath the hot, the very hot, Paris sun. He sat on a bench overlooking the Seine, where it was cooler. *Bateaux mouches* lay inertly alongside the quays beneath, awaiting the night when their passengers would embark to see Paris by moonlight, or lamplight, stuffing their way through too many courses of dinner as they stared. Or gawped, since most would be Americans, the only ones who could afford the fares – the only *white* ones anyway. Hedge didn't entirely consider Germans and Dutch and Belgians or even Frenchmen white, and as for Arabs . . . what a bunch! And everyone in Paris was currently sinister, to be suspected of evil intent, possible killers of the two most important persons in the British cabinet. Hedge felt his responsibilities keenly; but Roberts-White had blandly assured him that all was in hand, everything under full control and that he, Hedge, was far better employed in keeping his eyes and ears open around Paris rather than attempting to operate from within the Embassy. Hedge had been furious and still was; the simmer was not from the sun alone. But at the same time he had felt oddly relieved, since if there was to be any further contretemps at least he couldn't be held responsible. And Roberts-White had been pretty decent; he had referred admiringly to the business of the dead man in the hole, saying that Hedge had done very well indeed and there was one villain the less to worry about, though perhaps it was a pity he hadn't lived to be questioned. That thought was now very much with Hedge, worryingly so. The Head of Security might consider he'd run away rather fast, rather too precipitately, but his counter to that would be that it had been he who had been there and not the Head, and after all he wasn't Shard. He wasn't a fisticuffs man. Shard was. And damn it all, Hedge thought angrily by the banks of the Seine, in a sense he was doing a policeman's job now. Keeping his eyes and ears open. *Keeping obbo*. It wasn't really consistent with his dignity. Confound Shard.

However, he had dealt with Shard. With the PM in the offing, Shard was needed urgently in Paris. Hedge had been firm, very firm indeed: Roberts-White was to have Shard contacted and brought back, under FO orders, from dalliance with WDC Brett in the Ardèche. Alexander Vernodski hadn't been the only villain; plenty of others would take his place now. If only he had more information . . .

* * *

Shard and Eve Brett had been propelled in front of Tex's gun, away from little fat Annie to a far corner of the field. Behind Tex, Tom Tit and the skinhead Frigger had come up, and they had been given their orders: the hippies were to be kept clear. Frigger said most of them were high anyway and wouldn't be taking notice, and that appeared to be true. The field looked like an opium den, with recumbent bodies all over, possibly dreaming of the paradise to come when the UFO's zoomed in like big dinner-plates to take them on a different kind of trip. Reaching the secluded corner, Tex told Shard and Eve to turn round.

They did so; Tex held the gun very steady. He asked, "So what goes on between you and little fat Annie?"

"Any reason why I shouldn't talk to her?" Shard asked.

"Well, now, I don't know the answer to that, do I? Suppose you tell me, huh?"

"And if I don't – if I say it's nothing to do with you?"

Tex grinned. His face was an unpleasant one, and there was an intensity in the eyes, a curious light . . . he said easily, "Why, this," and he jerked the gun closer to Shard.

"Out here in the open?"

62

"Why not? People die, don't they?"

"And others ask questions."

"Not here they don't. There's no check on numbers, names. Graves are easy dug. The hippies, they do what I tell them."

Coolly Shard asked, "What's your game, Tex? The UFO thing's just a blind, isn't it, cover? What for?"

Tex said, "Not your concern, feller. Just tell me about your conversation, okay?" He paused. "And another thing. What brings you here, feller? Little fat Annie?"

Shard shrugged. "I like the sun. I like the freedom."

"And you don't believe in the UFOs?"

"No more than you do," Shard said evenly.

Tex moved fast. His free hand shot out like a snake, palm flat, and took Shard hard across the face, first one side then the other. Blood ran from cuts made by a heavy ring. Shard stood fast: the gun was still steady and the mad look in Tex's eyes seemed to be hovering on the brink. Without looking round Tex said, "Where's that faggot?"

"Here," Tom Tit said.

"Go get little fat Annie."

Tom Tit flounced away. Tex said, "Now we'll see what she has to say."

6

Little fat Annie came obediently, a big happy smile on her broad features. She was peasant-like and she was trusting. Shard liked her face; there was no guile there. He believed she could be easily led, and there was no doubt about it she fancied Tex. Physically the American was superb; tall, hefty, rippling muscles, even handsome if you could leave out the ice that from time to time replaced the weird blaze in the eyes. Or maybe that was part of the charisma that, for the hippies, he seemed to possess.

On arrival she curtseyed to him. Very olde worlde, but then he was God to these people. The curtsey did strange things to her flapping garment; when she stood up again there was a ruck. She didn't bother to smooth it down. Shard believed she was ready now and didn't in the least mind an audience, but Tex wasn't in the mood, having other matters on his mind. He backed away a little so that he was covering all three – Shard, Eve, little fat Annie.

Tex smiled at the girl. She responded. He said, "Now, Annie. Just tell me what this guy's been talking to you about, huh?"

She said, "Mikhail."

Tex looked blank as if the name meant nothing, but Shard detected interest. "So?"

"Simon was asking about Mikhail's mother."

"Yeah? Anything else, Annie?"

She said, "Oh yes. About Stanislav Asipov."

Tex didn't like that. The ice was back in his eyes. He said, "Tell me, Annie. All about it, right?"

She did; not that there was much to say. But it was enough for Tex. He swung round on Shard, face belligerent. "Just give me the low-down on who you are," he said savagely. "Who you are and where you fit – right?"

Shard stared back at him. "I'm no-one that would interest you," he said, shrugging. "I'm just a – "

"Just a hippy?"

"That's right."

"We'll see about that," Tex said. He nodded at Frigger. The skinhead's tongue came out and he licked his lips, enjoying his forthcoming role. He moved closer to Shard, giving a preliminary swing to his spiked metal ball, then jerked it hard towards Shard's legs. Shard dodged aside and the ball just missed: it swung again, this time striking the rear of little fat Annie, who gave a shrill scream. Tex scowled across at Frigger, his attention momentarily diverted, and Shard took his chance: he flung himself bodily on the American and Tex went down flat and winded. Shard wrenched the gun from his hand, covering him as he made to get back on his feet. Then both Frigger and Tom Tit came in. Something, not the spiked ball, took Shard on the back of his head and he went out, down deep. He didn't hear the oncoming police whistles or the ferocious barking of Alsatians as they bounded with their handlers over the recumbent hippies.

★　　　★　　　★

The local police had been in two minds when the message reached them from the *Police Judicaire* in Paris that they were to go in and get a man out from the hippie compound. On the one hand they were delighted to have a cast-iron order to break the place up; there had been so many complaints but nothing they could really make use of. On the other hand, the place was so appalling and they might catch all manner of diseases from the filth or even from so much as touching the inmates, all of whom were bound to have a loathsome disease in one form or another, very likely the incurable AIDS. However, once in they made a job of it. Hippies ran screaming in all directions, clutching discarded clothes. Batons were used freely, and it proved difficult for the dogs to be held back. So much potential meat. Little fat Annie, rooted with

65

her sore bottom to the spot near where Shard had fallen, was captured with ease and bundled back to a waiting police van with Shard and Eve Brett. Both Shard and Eve were being treated as hippies, despite Eve's loud protests. A number of other arrests were made; but in fact most of the commune's inmates got away, moving with astonishing speed. Among those that got away was Tex; Tom Tit and Frigger went into the bag. Frigger would be charged with murder; he had laid about himself maniacally with his spiked ball, and four of the policemen had had their heads stove in. As a result the others were savage and in no mood to listen to explanations from Eve Brett, not until she had battered them with the name of Simon Shard. It then penetrated that the man they had been sent in to get was lying on the floor of their van, injured.

After that no time was lost in getting the English detective into the hands of the medics at Bourg St Andéol. Shard had come to by the time they got him to the hospital and was anxious to reach Paris, but the doctors insisted on going through their routines. After all, he had a head injury and forms in triplicate stood like a paper moat between him and free movement northwards. However, he was able to instruct WDC Brett to contact the Paris Embassy and in due course the word came from the Prefecture of Police itself: Shard was to be flown out for the capital immediately, if necessary with a doctor and nurse in attendance. Shard had been confident of nothing less; Hedge would have given orders and would never have bothered himself with any thought for Shard's head. His own was much more important and it could be on the chopping block already. When Shard was unwillingly released, he found the local police chief in attendance. He said, "I'd like those two, the ones called Frigger and Tom Tit, to come with me. Also the girl."

"Tom Tit yes. The girl yes. Frigger no."

"But look – "

"Frigger no. There has been murder of my gendarmes. The man stays."

"Paris is going to need him."

The police chief was firm. He was very French and somewhat old-fashioned: moustachios twirled, there were overtones of Pétain, even of General Gamelin. "Frigger no. He will of course be questioned and the Prefecture in Paris will be informed, this I promise."

Shard had to leave it at that. Tom Tit might provide some of the answers; he had seemed close enough to Tex. With a hunt in progress for the American, Shard with his WDC, Tom Tit and little fat Annie was airlifted into Paris by a military helicopter and by a late lunch time was closeted with Hedge in a pew at the back end of Notre Dame. Having earlier tended to sneer at Roberts-White for his air of cloak-and-dagger, Hedge had had second thoughts and in any case had always really rather liked cloak-and-dagger so long as he was the instigator of it. And things were getting tricky now. He told Shard about the PM's decision to come over; Shard agreed that this toughened Security's job. This point put over, he had to listen to a long moan from Hedge about the dreadful night he had endured but had very successfully overcome. Shard pointed out unkindly that the hole in the pavement had been purely fortuitous.

"Oh, nonsense!" Hedge snapped. "Even if it was, I made good use of it you'll agree. You'd better make your report."

In the light of flickering candles Shard did so, under the cover of prayer, the two of them reverently kneeling as the tourists drifted past, gawping as usual. He told Hedge that Tex had reacted to his, Shard's, interest in Asipov. He went on, "There's a lot more behind Tex – he more or less admitted the UFO thing was just cover and I doubt if he has any real use for the poor deluded hippies, they're just part of the cover, of course. Or were. They're mostly scattered now."

Hedge gave a heavy sigh. Notre Dame he found depressing, even foreboding. Oddly perhaps, it reminded him of the French Revolution and of the fact that he was inside a land of incipient regicides and that soon now both the Prime Minister and the Foreign Secretary would also be there, representing monarchy. All that past terror and the streets of Paris running with blood . . . Hedge gave himself a shake. All that was a long time ago. He asked, "Where is this Tom Tit?"

"Police custody."

"We'd better talk to him. Or you had. Call upon me only as a last resort – you know what I mean, don't you, Shard? If you need more weight – but I doubt if you will. Tom Tit . . . he doesn't sound to me like a very strong character from your description."

Shard disagreed; Tom Tit, he believed, had a streak of hard steel in him and never mind the poncy bottom-waggling. But he didn't say this to Hedge, who wouldn't have listened in any case. Hedge went on, for no apparent reason, to say that he had had every help, or the Embassy had, from the French police and security people. It was surprising, his manner seemed to say, but it was the fact. They'd lost no time in hooking Shard away from the hippie commune, for one thing. It was very creditable and it was a relief to Hedge to know that they were taking the visit of the British VIPs so seriously. When the PM and the Foreign Secretary arrived in three days' time, there would be almost more plain clothes men than sightseers.

"I'm worried about the Americans," Hedge said. "The tourists, you know."

"Why?"

"The man Tex is an American, you said."

"Yes, true. But all Americans aren't Tex. However, I do see your point, Hedge."

"You'll bear it in mind, then?"

"Oh, yes, I'll do that."

Hedge glared. "It's all very well your saying that, Shard. What, precisely, are you going to *do*?"

"Talk to three people for a start," Shard answered. "Tom Tit, little fat Annie, and Frigger if necessary."

"He's still in Bourg St Andéol, isn't he? I'd sooner you didn't leave Paris again, Shard. Paris is where the trouble is going to come." Hedge shifted about on his knees, easing first one then the other. The Notre Dame hassocks were far from comfortable after a while. They had had quite a long pray and if they overdid it they would attract attention if only from a prowling priest who might feel it his duty to urge them into a confession box. Hedge muttered that he was going back to the Embassy, where he could be contacted if necessary and never mind Roberts-White. Then he got stiffly to his feet and sidled out of the pew. Shard gave it a few more minutes and then left himself, coming from the gloom of the cathedral into the bright sunshine of late afternoon. A boat on the Seine beckoned, a peaceful trip with Eve Brett beneath an awning and the ripple of the river on either hand. Dismissing useless urgings, Shard headed for police HQ, where he encountered WDC Brett who had had a preliminary talk with little fat Annie.

"Useful?" Shard asked.

"Not particularly, sir." Formality was back now, hippie-dom except for dress a thing of the past, at least for the time being. It was obvious that WDC Brett preferred it that way; she knew where she stood and there was a chasm between their ranks even though Shard always put her at her ease. "She told me she'd met Mikhail Kolnisenko, or Asipov, in Paris on her way back from London – "

"Had she indeed," Shard said. *"Met* him? *In Paris?* So he did get out of Russia . . . maybe that *is* why he wanted to contact his mother, as she suggested."

Eve said, "Our information is that he'd sort of rejected her, sir."

Shard nodded. "Right, it is. But he did want to get in touch, didn't he? However. So little fat Annie met Mikhail. Was this a chance encounter?"

"Apparently. She was very surprised – or so she said. Somehow she didn't quite convince me." WDC Brett paused. "She said she fell for him this time round. He'd grown up a lot . . . she found him very attractive."

"She's man mad, is little fat Annie. I thought Tex was the source of her sunlight. What about the boy friend who went with her to London?"

"No account, sir. Just a meal ticket for the journey."

Shard nodded again. "You've done well to get that much," he said. "I'll be seeing what a little pressure will do. But

I'll start on Tom Tit. We'll let little fat Annie stew for a while."

*   *   *

Tom Tit was not in an interrogation room; he was in a cell. He had, in English terms, resisted arrest after offering combat against the police. Also, he could be an accessory to the fact of Frigger's killing of police officers. He was not popular; to prove this he carried an egg-shaped, discoloured lump on his forehead. Before entering the cell, Shard viewed him through the spy-hole in the door. Tom Tit was sitting on a hard wooden plank fitted into the brickwork, his head in his hands, eyes staring at the floor. The thin lips were curved downwards and they were trembling as though he was about to burst into tears. Maybe the steel wasn't so well tempered, could be on the verge of metal fatigue, but time would tell.

The door was opened up and Shard went in alone. The door was shut behind him, and locked. Outside, two police-men stood guard. Tom Tit's head came up. Shard said, "You may have gathered already, I'm no hippie. I'm a detective chief superintendent, of the Metropolitan Police basically. I – "

"I'm a British subject," Tom Tit said. "These French bastards, they've got no right to hold me – "

"They have every right. Don't look to me to help you out. I saw what Frigger did to little fat Annie, remember? And you're part of the set-up. Number Two, you said. For my money, you've got form back home."

"I never."

"Well, we'll soon see. Your prints have gone to the Yard, Tom Tit. That'll take time. Meanwhile I'm in a hurry. If you come clean it could go in your favour. I think you know what I mean. Your past record and connexions could be useful, but it's Tex I'm interested in."

Tom Tit said viciously, "Get stuffed." He almost spat the words at Shard.

Shard shrugged. "It's up to you," he said. "I'm offering to

70

smooth your path. You're in for a rough ride, you know that. Accessory to murder. . . the French are going to throw the book at you. If you're prepared to talk about certain things that I believe may happen through the agency of your friend Tex, well, then the French might be persuaded to go a little easy. There are bigger fish than you currently about to give them a headache, one they don't want. At any price. Get me, Tom Tit?"

"I don't know what you're talking about." Tom Tit pouted.

"You don't? Then let me enlighten you." Shard stared down at Tom Tit and proceeded to take his brief well beyond his present knowledge. "There's a threat to the lives of the Prime Minister and the Foreign Secretary after they arrive in Paris. I know it. You know it. So do yourself a favour. Tell me about Tex."

He tried not to show his utter astonishment when Tom Tit burst into a peal of laughter. It was hysterical but even so it carried some sort of conviction. Tom Tit was genuinely amused at a total misconception. Shard knew he had thrown away what might have been a good hand. His basic ignorance of the facts was now all too clear to Tom Tit. An avenue had closed itself. Inwardly Shard cursed himself, but he kept a good front. He said, "All right, then. Have it your way. But when little fat Annie opens up I've a hunch she's going to cook your goose for you."

He backed to the door and knocked on it. It was opened up, locked again after he emerged. He told the officers he wanted to talk to the girl. He was taken to an interrogation room; there were currently no charges against little fat Annie, who in a painful sense was the victim. He found her sitting gingerly on the bandages applied in Bourg St Andéol, but otherwise placid and happy. She was so bovine . . . Shard said he hoped she was feeling better.

"Thank you, yes."

"Good." Shard sat down, facing the girl across a plain scrubbed table. "Now, you've spoken to my WDC – to Miss Brett. You'll know who I am."

"Oh, yes," she said. "I know. A policeman from London."

71

He nodded. "Do you know why I'm here – why I went to the commune?"

"No?" She sounded curious to know. Shard wasn't going to tell her yet. He asked her about Tex, attaching no strings or suggestions to the question.

"He is God," little fat Annie said with simplicity.

"Yes, so I understand. Can you tell me a little about his divinity, Annie?"

She said, "He exalts the soul. He lifts it up."

"In a UFO?"

It was meant to be sardonic; but little fat Annie nodded vigorously and happily. She had no worries, no doubts, life had been ironed out for her. Death was not to be feared; when the time came the UFOs would lift all the believers to paradise.

"What's paradise?" Shard asked, baffled by stupidity.

"So many things. It is individual."

"How?"

She said with that candid simplicity that was obvious manna to Tex's ambitions, "Each person – he or she makes his or her own paradise by his or her desires. If the soul strains after the desire, it is given in paradise."

"That's what Tex says?"

"Yes."

"Uh-huh. And your desires, Annie?"

She said, "Sex."

"Ah. So in paradise – "

"In my paradise all will be sex. Day and night, all the time, sex. It will be so wonderful."

"And it'll be the same for all the believers?"

She nodded. "Yes. According to the soul's desires, yes. But I think mainly sex, which is the desire of most."

"And all the hippies in that commune – they're all believers in Tex?"

"Yes, all of them."

"And you still are?"

"Of course, yes."

"You've not asked yourself why he hopped the twig?"

She seemed puzzled. "Hopped the twig?"

"Did a disappearing act, Annie. Left you all to face the police. Had you thumped on the backside. Doesn't it all sort of disturb your faith?"

"Oh, *no*," she said with confidence. "He will have his reasons. He is the important one, the one who must be preserved. When your Jesus Christ came down to earth, he was persecuted – "

"There are differences," Shard pointed out. "He never left anyone in the lurch. But are you saying that Tex came down to earth, like – "

"Yes, that is what I say. He has been there. That is why he *knows*, you see. He is another son of the same God. He has described it all to everyone."

"To each a different story, according to the individual desires?"

"Oh, yes," she said. "In the house of the father – "

"Tex's father?"

"Yes. In his house are the many mansions. But as I have said to you already, chiefly sex."

Shard nodded. He said, "I'm sure you have a very happy life with all that to look forward to. I'll accept your belief, Annie. Now let's talk about something else, shall we? Mikhail, natural son of Stanislav Asipov. I gather you met him in Paris not long ago. I'd like to know all about that."

Mikhail, too, was wonderful, Annie said. So beautiful, so strong, so sweet, with such good friends, also Russian. She loved Mikhail, she told Shard, sounding passionate. More, he asked, than she loved Tex? Oh, no. A different kind of love, an earthly one. Her love for Tex was on a different plane, basically the one the UFOs would one day fly to. There was no inconsistency at all, no more than there was in a wife loving her husband as well as loving God. Shard accepted that point with a wry face and pressed Annie about Mikhail and his friends.

A picture of a sort began to emerge.

*　　*　　*

73

Shard rang the Embassy from police HQ. He got Hedge, who sounded twittery and anxious. Yes, they would meet. Not in the Embassy, better if Shard didn't show his face around there, and not, this time, in Notre Dame. In the gardens flanking the Champs Elysées and facing the US Embassy in the Rue Boissy-d'Anglas there was a public lavatory.

"Dangerous," Shard said, tongue in cheek.

"I don't mean *in* it," Hedge snapped. "Near it there's a bench. I'll be reading *Paris-Match* – "

"Just in case I don't recognise you?"

Hedge slammed the receiver down. Shard left police HQ and arrived at the bench before Hedge, who had had a shorter walk, but there was a reason for his delay as he explained when he puffed up clutching *Paris-Match* like a baton. "Might have been followed, don't you know, so I took a very wide detour." The bench was a back-to-back affair and that was how they talked, not without some difficulty.

Shard said, "We're close to the American Embassy, Hedge."

"So what?"

"The Americans may get the blame, you may be thought one of theirs."

"I don't give a damn about the *Americans*," Hedge said crossly, "and I hope I'm not in the least likely to be mistaken for one in any case. What have you found out?"

"Firstly that little fat Annie's a sex maniac – "

"Not important, Shard."

"Just as you say, Hedge. What I found out was this: Mikhail's not alone in Paris. There was some dangerous work somewhere along the Baltic coast, then a sea trip. Normandy beaches. Being a non-person is a powerful incentive to taking a big risk to get out of the Soviet Union, it seems. Mikhail has a number of his non-person mates with him . . . apparently it's not uncommon in Russia for the paperwork to get ballsed up – "

"*Not* that expression, please!"

"All right. The point is, Mikhail didn't want Tex to get to

know he was in Paris. Little fat Annie was to be very careful about that."

"Why?"

"That didn't emerge."

"Well, it should have." Hedge was pettish. "Didn't you press?"

"Of course. But she didn't know. He hadn't said. I believe her. For one thing, she's too damned thick. . . for another, she's honest. She's a very nice girl, Hedge. I mean that. Her visit to Ernestine Kolnisenko was a genuine good deed. She wanted to help both Mikhail and his mother."

"I don't see how someone who's sex mad can be considered very nice. Perhaps that point was germane after all."

Shard grinned to himself. He said, "Well, I don't know, Hedge. I had a word earlier with Roberts-White. That hole in the pavement – he had some theories about your – "

"Thank you, Shard, that'll do." Hedge's tone was icy; behind Shard's back his face grew red. "You don't seem to have found out very much, do you? Dragging me out here at risk of being seen, you must be crazy."

Shard said, "I've not found out much yet, I agree. But I aim to do so. I need your preliminary help. Your word, you know – it carries weight."

"Yes."

"More than mine, with the French authorities."

"No doubt, no doubt, but – "

"They won't release little fat Annie."

"Good gracious, I should think not!"

"They're not making charges, but they regard her as helping with their enquiries – "

"Quite right, Shard."

"Perhaps. But not if you want to protect our VIPs. I assume you do."

"I do dislike rudeness, Shard. You're so uncouth at times, don't imagine for one moment it's lost upon me."

"Quite. Get her set loose, Hedge. We have a lot to find out. Little fat Annie can give us a lead."

Hedge blew out his breath. "Oh, dear! How?"

"Because once she's free, she'll be liable to be contacted by two persons: Mikhail, and Tex. When she is, I want to be around. And we haven't much time left, have we, Hedge?"

7

Hedge had been persuaded; it had not been a difficult task. In his mind little fat Annie was expendable and if things went wrong for her it wouldn't matter much. Back in the Embassy he made telephone contact with police HQ. When the police spoke rapid French at him and sounded unco-operative, he passed them over to Roberts-White. The First Secretary, a tactful man with high-ranking contacts inside the Préfecture, achieved the desired result. Little fat Annie would be released and a very discreet tail would be put on her. The local radio would help: an announcement would be made in the news broadcasts that the woman brought in from the hippie commune in the south had been freed by the police. When he had cut the call Roberts-White asked Hedge where the girl was expected to live.

"That's her problem," Hedge answered.

"But she hasn't any money."

"How do you know that?"

"The police said so. Also, she's going to be told to remain in Paris – "

"With no address given?" Hedge clicked his tongue. "What a country. How fortunate one isn't French! You'd better ring them back and tell them to provide her with cash, recoverable from the Embassy – "

"But she's not *British*, Hedge. She's Russian. I can't author-ise any disbursements for a Soviet citizen." Roberts-White gave Hedge a sardonic look. "Of course, I could always ask the Russian Embassy for help, I suppose."

Hedge snapped, "Oh, don't be ridiculous." He had no other suggestions to offer and the net result was homelessness for little fat Annie. Hedge was not worried; she was of loose morals and would cope. Roberts-White passed further information gleaned from the police: the girl would be told to report daily and her Soviet passport, in the name of Annie Glemko, had been impounded until further notice. Hedge ordered a check to be made on Annie Glemko with Whitehall; she had, after all, been in Britain recently and would have needed a visa. But when the reply came back it seemed that Whitehall knew nothing of interest concerning anyone named Glemko.

*　　　*　　　*

Shard knew he was being something of a bastard; playing with a girl's safety, possibly for all he knew with her life, was not a thing to be lightly undertaken. But he had his job to do and the security of the PM and the Foreign Secretary had to be paramount. He was developing a theory as a result of his talk with little fat Annie: Mikhail Asipov/Kolnisenko could be the key. Mikhail was in Paris with a number of other young men and women, non-persons as he had told Hedge. Tom Tit had seemed to find it funny that Tex should have any designs on the safety of the British VIPs; Tex according to little fat Annie was not to know that Mikhail was in Paris – but earlier, back in the commune in the Ardèche, Tex had not appeared to know who Mikhail was. That could have been a mendacious act. Probably was. Anyway, Tex and Mikhail appeared to be on opposite courses. In simple terms, one might be the goodie, the other the baddie. But Shard could see no likely connexion between either of them and the VIPs due in so soon from London.

Everything was yet to be found out.

In the meantime Shard was still dressed as a hippie and that might have its advantages. Eve Brett was similarly disguised; and together they could fade into the background of the Paris streets until the police made contact. This they would do by means of a pocket transceiver. Shard, who had conceived the idea of freeing little fat Annie before he had left police HQ to meet Hedge, had made a generalised and successful plea for the means of personal radio contact; the transceiver was in the hippie-type bag slung from his shoulder. Hedge, who knew

78

this, would have passed the word for Shard to be contacted the moment little fat Annie looked like becoming a helpful lead. Nothing was likely to happen yet. Shard drifted along towards the Champs Elysées, one of a crowd. He had arranged to contact WDC Brett by telephone after he had finished with Hedge; in the meantime she would be having further words with little fat Annie prior to the latter's release. Woman to woman, things could emerge, little things that might prove important. Finding a telephone, Shard called HQ: WDC Brett would rendezvous outside the Metro at Champs-Elysées Clemenceau in half an hour.

★　　　★　　　★

Little fat Annie was on top of the world. She hadn't minded the police; the English policewoman had been nice and friendly and they had chatted amicably until release had come. It was nice to be free . . . Paris was so beautiful and the shops were wonderful. It was hot but little fat Annie didn't mind that. She drifted along, smiling at all the world, placid, cowlike, thinking about Tex, but thinking without anxiety. Tex would be all right; Tex was immortal, untouched by what happened on earth. Soon they would all come together again in another happy hippie commune. She felt this in her bones. Her only worry was the divergence between Mikhail and Tex, the fact that she had a secret from Tex in regard to Mikhail. She felt an abounding love for them both and she wished they were friends; she would like Mikhail to join the commune, ideally. Then his mother could come over from England and they would both be happy, happy in Tex. That was, if it hadn't been for this secrecy . . .

Little fat Annie was utterly unaware of the police tail behind her. A long, thin plain clothes man with a lugubrious face, dyspeptic looking, almost ulcerous. Five o'clock shadow in plenty and a disagreeable twist to his mouth due partly to his stomach and partly to his wife's nagging: she didn't like being married to a policeman and wanted him to resign and join his father-in-law in running a *patisserie* in Montmartre. This, Pierre Desbans resolutely refused to do, even though he was

79

himself disenchanted with police life. *Patisseries* meant too much pastry by the very nature of their business, and Montmartre was a den of thieves and sin and his father-in-law was a very horrible man with a wife who nagged more than Marie. As a result of his refusal, Marie had begun to apply sanctions against him but at the same time was satisfying her natural desires with other men, men whom she flaunted at him brazenly, saying that it would stop only at the *patisserie*. If she was not careful, Marie would one day find her throat cut or strangled . . .

Preoccupation was bad for the concentration. After a while Pierre Desbans became aware that he had lost the girl. He gazed about in panic, put on speed, his stomach growing very bad with worry. It was no use; she had gone. He was a tail without a dog.

He halted, jostled by the crowd. He said, "*Merde!*" and then reached into his pocket for his transceiver.

*　　　*　　　*

The report, very apologetic, reached Shard via his transceiver and was also passed to Hedge in the British Embassy. Hedge was livid, all his deep feelings about foreign inefficiency proved right as he had known they would be.

"Can't be trusted to boil an egg!" he raved.

Roberts-White was less moved. He said, "Well, it's a pity, I suppose, but – "

"Pity! Good God, man, don't you realise . . . the PM – "

"We don't know there's any connexion, Hedge, it's really no more than conjecture."

"*Conjecture?* Asipov – Kolnisenko – this ridiculous Tex – "

"Yes, yes, Hedge, I do understand all that, I assure you. But really I fail to see how a lunatic who believes in UFOs can possibly be a threat – "

"That's not the point! The point's this fat girl and the man Mikhail." By this time Hedge had convinced himself that he had put Shard on the right track, all his own idea. He was seeing all manner of nasty happenings in the Paris streets, or even at the airport notwithstanding that the police presence would be so immense – even in the Presidential palace, even in the National Assembly. Of course it was French responsibility primarily to guard their guests but if anything went wrong the heavens would descend upon himself as well. "What are the fools doing about it, Roberts-White?"

"There's a full scale search, Hedge."

"A fat lot of good that'll be!" Hedge padded furiously about the room, this way and that, cheeks wobbling. "Shard ought to have done the job himself – the tailing. It's very remiss of him."

Roberts-White started to put Hedge's earlier thought into words. "The French – it's their – "

"Oh, damn and blast the French, Roberts-White, all this is far too dangerous to allow stupid protocol or national feelings to stand in the way of efficiency. For two pins, I'd tell them so!"

Roberts-White pointed. "There's the telephone, Hedge."

Hedge stopped and stared. "What? Oh, don't take up everything I say, my dear fellow. Get Shard here."

"I can't."

"No, but the French police can, they're in contact with him. Ring them and get them to pass the word."

*   *   *

Little fat Annie knew precisely where she was going. She had no money; something had to be done about that, and Mikhail was the obvious answer. She didn't know Mikhail's actual whereabouts but she had met him in Montmartre and he had seemed familiar with the district and appeared to be known to the proprietor of a café opposite the steps leading up to the Sacré Coeur. It was possible he might visit that café; it was her best hope in any case. It was a long walk but little fat Annie set out with a smile on her face. When she got there, with no money to buy coffee and thus entitle herself to a seat at one of the pavement tables, she sat on the ground opposite and waited expectantly. She waited a long time and there was no sign of Mikhail; she decided it would do no harm to ask the café proprietor if he had seen Mikhail lately. She got to her feet and crossed the road and in so doing bumped into a young Chinese. She gave him a happy smile and said she was sorry. The Chinese moved back with her to the pavement; they were pushed against each other by the crowd, and Annie smiled again, giggling a little.

The Chinese smiled back engagingly. He had little French but some things were universal, like little fat Annie's smile of welcome. He used such French as he knew. "Jig-a-jig?" he said.

Well, why not? Money didn't grow on trees. "Yes," little fat Annie said.

"You have place to go?"

"No . . ."

"Then come." Montmartre hotels were broad-minded, more so than those in Peking. Little fat Annie went, and emerged a hundred francs richer. But it wasn't just that: she could scarcely believe her luck. Leaving the bedroom and going down the sleazy stairs she saw a man coming up and the man was Mikhail. It was astonishing. She fell upon him lovingly. He lived right there, he said. He took her to his room.

The trail, so far as the French police were concerned, had gone dead. It was equally dead so far as Shard was concerned; nil reports kept reaching the Embassy after he and Eve Brett had arrived in response to Hedge's urgent summons.

"You'll have to do something, Shard."

"It's an impasse right now. We haven't a single lead."

"It's not good enough, just to say that."

Shard turned to WDC Brett. "That matey talk with little fat Annie. Did *nothing* emerge?"

"Only what I've reported, sir. Which really came to nothing, yes."

Shard said grimly, "Let's go through it all again, shall we?"

They did, while Hedge suppressed his impatience angrily. It was still a nil result. Little fat Annie had just prattled on and on about the hippie commune and Tex's divinity. WDC Brett's opinion was that strictly the girl wasn't all there. She had tried to fix her mind on Mikhail, and there had been some prattle about him as a result, but nothing useful and no references as to where he might be. Maybe she wasn't so daft after all and was keeping certain relevant details to herself. WDC Brett had asked the question direct: where in Paris had she met Mikhail? But little fat Annie hadn't known Paris very well and she hadn't been able to be specific. WDC Brett had got no more out of her than had Shard. She had plenty of simple cunning.

Hedge asked, "What about that man?"

"Tex?"

"No, the other one – Tom Tit."

Shard nodded. "For what it's worth – seeing he's all we have – I'll try him again. But don't expect too much."

"I was thinking about the way he laughed when you spoke of a threat to the PM and Foreign Secretary. In my opinion you should have pressed him on that, Shard."

"For divers reasons," Shard said heavily, "it wasn't the most propitious moment. I intended making some capital out of little fat Annie first, then going back to him."

"I'd say you've missed your chance of that now."

"Not necessarily so. Tom Tit won't know the girl's been turned loose. But I say again, don't expect too much, then you won't be disappointed."

Shard left the Embassy with WDC Brett. He was hopeful, but not very, that the general call put out for little fat Annie might produce results. Someone just might have seen her around and widespread police questioning might dig that someone out. On the other hand, even though little fat Annie's physical construction stood out to some extent, she wasn't the only one of her build by a long chalk. Finding her now could be a hard slog.

Tom Tit produced nothing at first. Shard tried the old ploy of telling the man that little fat Annie had talked; Tom Tit didn't believe it. The girl didn't know anything.

"So there's something to know," Shard said.

Tom Tit lifted his eyebrows. "What makes you think that?" he asked, all innocence. "I just meant she didn't know anything. She's doolally, that's what I meant."

"Nicely covered," Shard said ironically. "I suppose you realise that if anything happens during the Prime Minister's visit, you're in the hot seat, right where we want you?"

"If anything happens while I'm inside," Tom Tit said, "I'll be in the bloody clear, duckie, and you know it."

"Conspiracy's a wide net," Shard said. "Don't doubt that we're going to nail you. Like I said before, talking could help to get you out from under. Just tell me what you know about Mikhail Asipov."

That brought a reaction from Tom Tit. His mouth twitched a little and his eyes narrowed. There was a wary look about him now. Shard was about to press and press hard when the cell door opened and a police officer came in. There was, he said, a telephone call for M'sieur Shard from the British Embassy. Shard caught Tom Tit's expression, which was quickly wiped away. He said, "I'll be back."

The call was from Hedge. Hedge sounded excited. He said, "There's been word from the Yard. That man's prints – Tom Tit's. He's got form, Shard, plenty of it. Just listen to this. It looks to me as though it's very relevant."

8

Shard had taken notes of what Hedge had reported. It was detailed, crimes and dates, the lot. Back in the cell Tom Tit stared at the piece of paper in Shard's hand. He didn't seem to like it.

Shard said, "You might have saved us the trouble. We were bound to find out as soon as your prints went in. Playing for time, were you?"

Tom Tit didn't answer.

Shard glanced down at his notes. "We never met but I've heard of you under your baptismal name – you weren't known as Tom Tit way back, right? That's recent, and I'd guess was given you by Tex. GBH – five years on the Moor. Robbery with violence, manslaughter, drunken driving, you did the lot right down to importuning for immoral purposes. Spent most of the last twenty years inside, released three months ago from the Scrubs. Check?"

"If you say so."

"Which was when you became a member of a mob called Communist Alliance Transatlantic – CAT."

Tom Tit's face had gone very still, totally expressionless. Shard said, "We know about CAT. We know what it stands for, what its aims are. Destruction of the Establishment, in brief. In America and the UK. Insidious . . . CAT's been behind ninety per cent of the strikes, trying to wreck the economy. You're in cahoots with the IRA, have links with the PLO – you don't, in fact, just stick to the transatlantic label. You've had other links – Baader Meinhof for one. Red Brigades. Spain, Italy, wherever there's communism to be encouraged." He paused, staring into Tom Tit's face. "I don't need to go on, do I? There's just one point: Tex's involvement. He's part of CAT, right?"

85

There was no response.

Shard said, "I put it to you again. Last time I did so, you laughed. I believe you and Tex are over here on a killing mission. The Prime Minister and the Foreign Secretary. Are you still laughing?"

Tom Tit said, "Like a drain." But he didn't laugh; there was fear in his eyes now. He said, "You got it wrong, dead wrong."

"Then you'd better put me right."

"I'm saying nothing."

Shard said steadily, "Once again I'll repeat myself. Being inside isn't going to help you if anything happens to the British delegation. You'll go down on a lifer for treason – remember what I said about conspiracy. And remember Tex is still on the loose. That's where the danger lies for you. Any help you can give will stand in your favour afterwards. All to lose, Tom Tit, and nothing to gain by withholding information now. I have to say that time's running out, but as for me, I'm a patient man and I'll wait."

*   *   *

Mikhail had been on the point of checking out from the hotel in Montmartre. Little fat Annie had made it just in time; in the bedroom as the young Russian pushed his gear into a canvas bag hanging from a shoulder strap, she looked at him with love. He was so thin, so hungry-looking, his face so gaunt and strained, he aroused a kind of mother instinct in the fat girl. He had aged since the days in Russia – she had noticed that the last time they had met here in Paris, so short a time ago. She reached out and stroked his cheek; irritably he threw off the hand.

"There is no time. I must go."

He spoke in Russian: the girl was pleased to hear the mother tongue again. Whatever life in Russia might be like, there was comfort in the familiarity of the language. She said, "I will come with you, Mikhail. We shall go together, wherever it is you go."

He turned and looked into her eyes. "No. There will be danger. I have so much to do."

"What is it you have to do, Mikhail?"

"I can't tell you that," he said. "You must leave me and go back to your commune."

"No," she said. She told him what had happened, that the hippies were all dispersed and that Tex had gone, she didn't know where, that she herself had been detained by the police. She could see he was shaken by the news about Tex.

He said, "Perhaps there is danger for you in that, Annie."

"From Tex? Oh, no."

"I say there might be. You know so little of Tex."

"And you, Mikhail, what do you know?"

"Enough," he said briefly. He wouldn't elaborate. Frowning, he paced the room, his mouth twitching with some nervous tic, dark hair falling over the long, narrow face. His mind was busy: little fat Annie could be his Achilles' heel if she was to be left on the loose in Paris. She knew too much about him, and she could be contacted by Tex. She wanted to go with him: he could read the love in her eyes. There might also be danger from the police. Mikhail made up his mind quickly.

"You shall come," he said.

She smiled with happy relief. "Where do we go, Mikhail?"

"Out of Paris." He told her no more; she didn't press. They left the bedroom hand in hand. Mikhail paid his bill and they went out into the sunlight and the Montmartre crowds, still hand in hand but walking fast. Down past the café where they had last met, past the eminence of Sacré Coeur, down a narrow street to turn left past cheap, tawdry shops to République Metro station. They emerged again into sunlight at Saint-Placide, not far from Hedge's hotel in the Rue de Vaugirard and, still walking fast, Mikhail led the way down a shadowed alley with a derelict warehouse at its end.

*   *   *

"He began to sweat," Shard said in the Embassy, "and then I had him."

Hedge was all agog. "You mean he cracked, Shard?"

"Right. He'd had enough of prison life. He wasn't far off grovelling for favours – "

"I trust you promised nothing?"

"No promises," Shard said. "But I'll expect co-operation to get him a hefty cut in his sentence. He's earned it."

"Your recommendation will be put forward," Hedge said pompously, "if *I* think his information's worth it."

"You will," Shard said. He lit a cigarette and blew smoke across the room. Hedge pointedly agitated the air with a pudgy hand. Shard repeated, "You will. And it's straightforward enough – up to a point, that is. We were right in one thing: it does concern the VIPs. They're at risk – "

"I always said so, Shard, did I not?"

"Yes, Hedge. But it's not quite *that* simple – "

"You just said – "

"Yes, I know, Hedge. But just listen. I know, now, why Tom Tit went into a peal of laughter when I suggested that first time that Tex was here on a killing mission against the international brass. He's here on a killing mission, that's true enough, but not the brass – "

"You said the VIPs *were* concerned, Shard."

Shard sighed. "Yes. Do listen, please. Tex is after Mikhail Asipov – "

"Goodness gracious!"

" – and Mikhail, according to Tom Tit, is after the Russian delegation."

Hedge had a mottled aspect. "The *Russians*? Oh, my God, Shard." He dabbed at his cheeks with a linen handkerchief. "Worse and worse . . . why the Russians? Did a reason emerge?"

"Only by way of conjecture. Tom Tit's not privy to what goes on in Mikhail's mind. But Tex fancied Mikhail and his mates want to hit back at the Soviet in revenge for the Soviet having made them into non-persons." Shard gave a shrug. "There may be more behind it than that, but we've yet to find out."

Like Tom Tit earlier, Hedge was sweating now. Never mind that he'd suspected assassinations all along, it was still a shattering thing to have confirmed . . . all those VIPs, Prime Minister, Foreign Secretaries from East and West, the brass from NATO and the EEC; hit the Russians and you were bound to hit some of them as well. Hoarsely he asked, "How did Tom Tit find this out, Shard?"

"Tex has his informers."

"That girl?"

"Little fat Annie? I don't think so. Unless perhaps by just being stupid and talking out of turn – *if* Mikhail confided in her, which is highly doubtful."

Hedge had found something to pounce on. "I thought you said Tex didn't seem to know who Mikhail was, in that commune?"

Again Shard shrugged. "He was just covering, that's all, trying to prise information out of the girl. I'd say that's obvious enough, wouldn't you?"

Hedge flushed angrily, but didn't otherwise react, there was too much worry around now. It was horrifying. Blame would speed in his direction if anything went wrong and he would be pilloried. His voice high he asked, "Have you no details of how the attempt's to be made?"

"None. In both cases, Tex against Mikhail, Mikhail against the brass. Tom Tit hadn't been confided in to that extent."

"The timing?"

"Ditto."

Hedge got to his feet and walked across to the window. Over his shoulder he said, "Asipov – the father, in London. Do you see any connexion, Shard?"

"No more than before."

"Oh dear, oh dear." Hedge used his handkerchief again and mopped at his face. His eyes, when he turned round, looked haunted. "This – this Tex business. What's his reason for wishing to kill Mikhail, do you know that?"

"Yes. The basic answer's CAT. Tex is acting to stop Mikhail getting at the Russians – "

"As simple as that?"

Shard said, "Tom Tit said so, but, again, like in Mikhail's case, there could be more behind it."

"And if there is, you don't know?"

Shard nodded. "Right, Hedge."

"I don't think," Hedge said heavily, "that this Tom Tit really helped very much. Oh, I agree he's positively alerted us and I'll be able to insist on a massive tightening of security, but – " He broke off; the internal telephone had burred. He went to the desk and answered; it was Roberts-White. Hedge nodded, looked tremendously excited and hopeful, said 'yes' a few times, then cut the call and turned to Shard.

"The girl," he said. "Likely sighting. The police have a report from a member of the public . . . they issued descriptions to café proprietors and so on. Possibly seen outside a café near Saint-Placide – "

"Not definite, then."

"Not definite, but helpful potentially. You'd better get along to police HQ, Shard, and stand by."

"I'll do that," Shard said. "I'd like to sort out one thing first, though. You and I are here for the security of the British delegation. The others aren't part of *our* brief. Once Tom Tit's information is passed on, Hedge, it becomes mainly a French show. It's their country and they'll take over. I – "

"What are you getting at, Shard?" Hedge was impatient. He was very conscious of passing time.

"This," Shard answered. "I'm going out on my own – if I establish contact with little fat Annie. I'm going back underground with WDC Brett once that happens. I'll hope not to cross any wires with the French security people, but there's always a chance I may. I'm asking for your backing in anything I decide to do."

Hedge dithered; this was the kind of decision he detested making. Shard's ideas could lead to trouble and difficulty; the French were such a curious lot, so unpredictable, so emotional, so unstable really. There would be so much Gallic froth and pandemonium as it was, once they knew of the threat on their precious soil. All sorts of people would vie with each other to take charge – for one, there was the National Gendarmerie Intervention Group, known for short as the GIGN. The French were very proud of the GIGN and the GIGN was very proud of itself and would insist that its men were the ones to cope – after all, this *was* an anti-terrorist project. Oh, dear.

Hedge sighed; the British were better at this kind of thing . . . and that, in a sense, was of course just what Shard was suggesting. And if he, Hedge, could bring this off successfully in spite of the French then it would be a tremendous feather in his cap . . .

Even so, Hedge temporised pompously. He said in a distant tone, "My dear Shard, I think I've always said I give my backing to all my officers when they're right – without fear or favour."

Shard, who had correctly observed the obvious mental processes and knew his man well, realised he had got all he was going to get and that he had got his point through.

*   *   *

At police HQ Shard was told that the sighting had been a brief one, made in passing. The café proprietor was, however, pretty certain the girl he had seen was little fat Annie. She was reasonably unmistakable; and she had been with a young man, a cadaverous-looking young man who had seemed in a hurry. They had gone along the Rue de Rennes in the direction of the Tour Montparnasse and after that the café proprietor had lost sight of them – profit was profit as the police must understand, and he had been busy with customers.

This report taken, Shard left HQ with Eve Brett and took the Metro to Saint-Placide. Emerging, they mingled once again with the crowds and sauntered towards the Tour Montparnasse, a skyscraper block that dominated Paris, almost putting the loftier Eiffel Tower in the shade of lean, skeletal tracery. Shard's mind was busy: he was thinking about the commune hippies. Just cover for Tex, as he'd thought – or more than that? They could just conceivably have some part to play in their drugged innocence, but what? In any case they were all dispersed now . . . Tex wouldn't go back to the commune for obvious reasons, and if the hippies had drifted back – the police in Bourg St Andeal had reported that some in fact had – they would presumably be lost to Tex.

And the method of assassination – Mikhail's method? That was, if Tex didn't get him first, which would be the best way out for all concerned, perhaps. Rifles, with telescopic sights? There was going to be a motorcade through the Paris streets and the spectators would be legion, but the Paris police and security men would be taking every possible precaution. Danger in the French Foreign Ministry where the meetings were to take place? That would be equally well taken care of. Not very propitious for a non-person or persons to choose as a killing ground. There had to be something else, some occasion when the VIPs themselves would be relaxing, perhaps, though they probably wouldn't get much chance of that, the schedule was pretty tight, a lot of business to be got through in a short time. International conferences, mini summits – and this looked like more than a mini summit – were not the times for fun and games . . .

A dinner?

There was going to be a dinner, naturally, given by the President of France in the Presidential palace, the Elysée, a posh affair – and of course very elaborately screened and guarded with plain clothes GIGN men among the flunkeys. Hardly a hope there, Shard would have thought.

They reached the skyscraper block. It began to look like a wild goose chase. Little fat Annie and her escort, who could be Mikhail, had gone well and truly to ground again.

"So what do we do?" Eve Brett asked.

"Hang around. It's all we've got. Care for a *café au lait*?"

"Yes," she said. They sat at a table in an establishment beneath the many storeys of the Tour Montparnasse and Shard ordered, sitting back and keeping a close eye on the crowds that drifted past along the street or in and out of a big store whose doors were immediately opposite the café. Taking into account the delay occasioned by the British Prime Minister he now had two days before the brass assembled – time nagged as it always did on jobs where there was a kind of deadline, an uncertain deadline which made it worse, and leads and facts remained obstinately concealed. The coffee finished, they got up and crossed the road and walked towards the Rue de Vaugirard and along it in the direction once again of Saint-Placide.

No little fat Annie – but Hedge, entering the Hotel Aviatic, having disembarked from a taxi that this time had managed to find the proper entry to the one-way street. Glancing to his right, Hedge spotted them, dithered, scowled, vanished, and then came out again and waited for Shard to come up.

He said, "I told you to *stand by*, Shard. Not show yourself. Are you mad?"

"No, Hedge. Little fat Annie has no fear of me, you know. She's not facing any charges – not so far as either she or we know so far."

"Yes, but – "

"And she's a simple soul. If she happens to see us, she'll come running."

"The man won't, if he's Mikhail Asipov."

"Agreed, if she tells him who we are."

"Well, then!"

Shard said equably, "Nothing's lost, Hedge. The fact that I'm around could force them into the open. Flush them out. Once they're on the move, that's when we have our best chance. Check?"

Hedge scowled again but didn't answer. Shard, grinning, said, "You don't want to get tainted with our brush, do you, Hedge? Being seen talking to us – you know?"

Suddenly, Hedge vanished back into the hotel foyer, his face red. Shard and WDC Brett moved on, not hurrying. A couple of hundred yards or so past the Hotel Aviatic they took a right-hand turn, came out into the road running from the Tour Montparnasse to Saint-Placide, the one they'd taken on emerging from the Metro. Just as they had turned down towards Saint-Placide there was a traffic accident, a car hit broadside by another emerging from a garage. It wasn't serious but there was a lot of shouting and fists were shaken. French fists – the hit car bore a British registration and its occupants were more phlegmatic. A crowd gathered, displaying interest, offering advice, shouting abuse at the British car. Shard reflected upon a facet of the Paris traffic scene that he had noted on previous visits as well as this current one: you never, or hardly ever, saw a British registered car except one that had been immobilised due to having been hit by a French one. But this was minor; he and Eve were already moving on when something more important happened: a girl recognisable immediately as little fat Annie appeared in the entry to a tatty building at the end of an alley that ran alongside the garage from which the French car had emerged. Just a brief glimpse before she disappeared again, but it had been enough.

Eve had seen the girl as well. Shard said, "I'm going in."

"On your own?"

He said, reaching for his transceiver, "I'll ask for plain clothes assistance, Eve. Get back to the Aviatic and warn Hedge."

She turned away for the Rue de Vaugirard. Shard made brief use of his pocket radio, shoved it back, and entered the alley cautiously. A cat overtook him, its tail high in the air. Nothing else moved and soon even the sounds from the street seemed muted. The buildings were high, a block of flats on one side, the garage and its workshops on the other. There was a smell of garbage, largely stale fish. The cat was bound for its source, a heap of rubbish near the dereliction of the building where Shard had spotted the girl – it was an abandoned warehouse, he saw. As he approached, a big door was drawn aside, running on rusty metal tracks. It had been opened from inside; Shard didn't see who was doing it, but he heard a car's engine start up. A moment later a door slammed and the car came out. It was a small one, a Fiat. It accelerated; as it came for him Shard saw little fat Annie in the front beside a dark, cadaverous man and after that he had to move fast for his life, very fast. Overhead there was a sort of gantry, a bar between two uprights. Shard jumped, got a grip, and heaved himself up as the car went fast beneath him. He heard a subdued phut-phut and bullets spattered the wall beside him, dislodging plaster. He remained intact; there were no more shots. The Fiat had gone out fast into the roadway, turning towards the Tour Montparnasse.

Shard dropped to the ground and ran for the road. The Fiat was already in the traffic stream having barged its way out, but it wasn't making much progress in the jam and he reckoned he could catch it up.

He ran. Something was snarling up the traffic ahead. A man who had been in the back of the Fiat got out, went round behind the car and just as Shard came up at speed he stepped forward, a hand raised in greeting, a smile of welcome on his face for the benefit of the passers by, and a foot outstretched. Shard went headlong. As the man bent over him in propagandic concern, he felt the hypodermic go into his arm.

★   ★   ★

The French had been fast, but not fast enough. They had sent in agents of the GIGN, which proved they were taking things seriously, but by the time they'd got there all was peace and quiet, the warehouse was deserted and no clues had, as yet anyway, been found. Impasse: and the British police officer had vanished. That was the only sure and certain thing about it. It was true – and very possibly relevant – that a knot of people in the street not far away from the alley had witnessed an unusual occurrence, a man falling head over heels and then being lifted inert into a small car, but that had been explained: he was a friend of the occupants and had been trying to catch up the car, and had unfortunately fallen and knocked himself out. He had not looked well; and the man, his friend who had lifted him to his feet, had been very concerned and had said they would take him straight to the hospital. The small car was a Fiat, and with the snarl-up cleared it had been driven away as fast as the traffic would allow, which of course in Paris was very fast, and no-one had thought of taking the number.

Hedge was livid. The hospitals had been checked and no-one had been admitted following a fall near the Tour Montparnasse. All Hedge's prophecies concerning French inefficiency had once again come true. It was obvious the man was Shard. Hedge was back in the Embassy now, having been contacted by Roberts-White not long after WDC Brett had reported Shard's intentions. WDC Brett was with him and was taking the brunt of his despair. Without Shard he was lost and in no mood not to complain about it.

"Too blasted impetuous!"

Eve said nothing but her face showed her concern for Shard and her dislike of hearing him criticised. Hedge raved on, pacing the floor, cheeks wobbling. The whole of France must be alerted, Shard must be found. Tactfully, Roberts-White agreed. All possible would be done. It would not, he also agreed, be long now before the VIPs swarmed in from points east and west. Yes, it was all very worrying. No, the French hadn't been as fast as they might have been, but now they were pulling out all the stops.

"Looking for a Fiat, number unknown, which'll almost certainly be changed for some other vehicle if they're going far. Really, it's *too* bad!"

★　　　★　　　★

Hedge had been right: the Fiat was ditched within an hour of leaving Paris. Mikhail Asipov, or Kolnisenko, had his contacts and his safe houses and there was always the chance that someone had noted the number of the Fiat. Shard was out for some while; he didn't come round until they had reached that first safe house near the Seine, some thirty miles north-west of Paris. It was a farm – that much he could smell when he returned to awareness on a sofa.

First he saw little fat Annie, who clasped her hands and said, "He is better, Mikhail." She said this in Russian. The next person Shard saw was Mikhail, dark, corpse-like, intense and dangerous.

In bad English Mikhail asked, "You know who I am?"

"I can guess. Mikhail Kolnisenko."

"Is right, yes."

"Or is Asipov more correct?"

"Is so, yes."

"Then you know? You know that – "

"Yes, I know. Do not move. Here is a man gunned."

"Really." There was; the man, with gun, moved into Shard's field of vision. He was unknown to Shard but he had a Russian look, an old-fashioned look, rather like Shard's idea of a Cossack of pre-revolutionary days. He was elderly, and there was a flowing moustache, white stained yellow with nicotine, and he had an aristocratic cast of countenance. Shard, who was feeling no after-effects from the drug, took the wind from the man's sails with a shrewd guess.

He said, "Avengers of St Petersburg, I presume?"

The man gave a start. Mikhail's face tightened up. The man said, "You know?"

"Yes. Vernodsky, now dead. Why did he shoot at Hedge?"

"To stop him," the man said.

"Quite. But why?"

"You are all the enemy, that is why."

"I thought your enemy was the Soviet leadership."

"So. This is true. But also those who try to stop our plans. Hedge we wished to question before he died. The shot was in fact not to kill at that moment. To wound only, and catch. Now, soon, we shall question you."

Shard stared at the Russian's face, and into the mouth of the gun he carried. It was much more than just a revolver; it was a Kalashnikov sub-machine-gun, with a rate of fire of something like six hundred rounds a minute. It wouldn't, of course, be silenced, but no doubt they were in a lonely spot. He said, "Just a moment. The Avengers of St Petersburg . . . does this explain how Mikhail's been able to build a set-up in France – which I assume he has?"

"Yes," the man answered. "Mikhail has all he needs. Men, weapons, radio, explosives. Co-operation from many French also, French who do not like the communist element in their own country and do not wish to see the extension of Soviet influence, which will come about if the summit meeting is successful."

"Why not leave it up to the British delegation to have it stopped?"

"No. This is the best way."

"It's the fool's way. Only the Soviet will benefit from an assassination. What about world opinion, French opinion too? Never mind your French anti-coms, they'll – "

"We know what we are doing." Steel had come into the voice and the eyes were blazing, like those of Tex back in the hippie commune. Shard shrugged; as ever, fanatics were impossible to penetrate. If this thing was to be settled by the gun, then he had to get the first shot in and that was all. He was about to speak again when a door opened and another man came in and announced, in French, that the van was ready and they all went out, with Shard ahead of the Kalashnikov. And less free than before: his wrists were tied behind his back. Outside the front door was a Dormobile, French number plates, big and comfortable. Shard had a brief glimpse of fields and, below a slope of the land, the water of the Seine. He didn't get a chance to study the terrain from the Dormobile's windows; he was put into the lavatory compartment and the door was locked on him. The window was a blank sheet of steel.

As soon as they were all in, the vehicle started off.

9

Later, things began to emerge and to some extent come full circle. The Dormobile was driven fast for some while – Shard, unable to look at his wrist-watch, was unable to estimate the time with any accuracy – and then stopped after slowing for some distance over very rough ground which caused the effluent in the Elsan beneath him to slop and gurgle – at least he'd had a seat for the journey. When he was brought out he was in an integral garage; he was taken through a door into a passage, and from there into what looked like a study – big desk, bookcases, telephone, filing cabinet. It could be the office of a self-employed professional man but there were no clues as to precisely what profession it might be. With his hands still tied, Shard was pushed into a chair and the Kalashnikov was placed on the desk, with the elderly Cossack, if such he was, not far from it. Shard looked through the room's one window: there wasn't much to be seen. In fact, just a blank wall, a garden wall with some kind of creeper growing over it.

"Now the questions," the Cossack said. He wanted to know how much had leaked to the British and French security people. It must have been obvious that quite a lot had; but Shard refused to answer any of the probing questions since even mendacious answers could well give away the fact that not enough had leaked. The Cossack lifted his Kalashnikov from the desk and said, "If you do not tell us, you will die."

"Maybe," Shard said indifferently. "Maybe not."

"How is this?"

"One always presumes the hostage is more use if kept alive."

The Russian laughed. "But you are not a hostage."

"Neither was Stanislav Asipov, presumably."

"What?" The man was puzzled. "I do not understand. Asipov had defected, he was in a British hospital, he was never in our hands – "

"And he was more or less on your side, he was anti the Soviet system or he wouldn't have defected. So why kill him, for God's sake?" Shard paused, staring into the Russian's eyes. "We know you did, you see. Vernodski's prints were found after the shooting. It doesn't quite add up – does it?"

The Russian glanced to his left, met Mikhail's eye. Something passed between them . . . and Mikhail had been the natural son of Stanislav Asipov. There would scarcely be any filial feeling for a man he had never, until the knowledge had come out, regarded as a father, a man he might hardly even have known, but Mikhail's face had registered something all the same. The Russian said. "Yes, his death was arranged by our organisation." He paused. "Perhaps you know of a telephone call made to your Foreign Office, to Hedge. A warning that Asipov would die if not handed back."

"Yes," Shard said.

"That call was a lying one, none of it true – it was made by evil persons known as Communist Alliance Transatlantic – "

"Tex!"

There was a nod. "Him, yes – not himself but one of his organisation. We knew of this too late, and then, you see, because we feared the British would believe it and might hand Asipov back on humanitarian grounds, we – "

"You got in first. Yes, I do see. But why were the Soviet authorities so keen to get him back?"

The Cossack shrugged. "Always they wish to get back a defector. But it was special in the case of Asipov, because, you see, he knew of our plans – "

"He was a member of the Avengers of St Petersburg?"

"Yes, that is so. For a long time something like this has been planned, and we awaited the opportunity which has now at last come. From it there will be no deflection. We are confident also that we shall succeed." He undoubtedly sounded it; and he, rather than Mikhail, seemed to be the boss. Shard wondered if he too was a non-person.

100

Shard put the question direct.

"No. I am not so unfortunate. For a long time I have lived in the political west, in France, where I was given asylum many years ago after the revolution – I was then a child, little more than a babe in my mother's arms. Mikhail Asipov has suffered much, and his friends also." The Russian used a phrase Shard had heard before, from Mikhail's mother. "They are the undead, those who have not the peace of the truly dead but are forced to live on without identity, without hope, without anything. But now their time has come to strike back in the name of all suffering Russians who are at the mercy of the Soviet system. And you shall help them now by answering my questions."

*　　　*　　　*

In official Paris there was a degree of the pandemonium that Hedge had expected from the French, a good deal of it sparked off by Hedge himself, his panic on hearing that Shard was missing having caused him to bypass both Roberts-White and His Excellency the Ambassador and project his panic down the telephone line to the French Foreign Ministry, the Police Judicaire and the Minister of State for Public Security, even though he much mistrusted the latter because his office sounded sinisterly like the revolutionary Committee of Public Safety presided over by the dreadful Citizen Robespierre who had instituted the Reign of Terror in 1793. As a result of his calls Paris seemed about to be obliterated under a snowstorm of initial letters, for all sorts of groups were now under suspicion, much greater suspicion than had up to now been the case. INLA, PLO, IRA, plus many others including Baader-Meinhof and Action-Directe and the Red Brigades, too short in full to warrant initials, jostled with NATO, EEC and GIGN. Everyone in Paris knew that the IRA plus INLA had been responsible for many past outrages in the capital, though they had masqueraded as something else, not caring whose banner they sullied, and that the PLO was inclined to support any faction with explosive aims. For their own reasons – to embarrass the west and France in particular – these groups might even connive at the killing of Russians and then blame the EEC. Terrorism had become a way of life. In a sense this was just one more threat and Paris was growing accustomed to such things; but this time it was big, and Hedge was stoking the fires.

Shard had to be found. No-one could contemplate the assassination of top Russian ministers on French soil. As ever, the missiles stood poised. They were everywhere on the west's perimeter. It was believed from Intelligence sources that upwards of 500 SS-20 medium-range missiles carrying up to 1500 warheads were deployed against Western Europe. The risk was immense. In the trigger-happy eighties anything could happen at any moment. Thank God, many people were saying fervently, the Americans were not involved on this occasion. The Minister of State for Public Security said as much to Hedge, on the telephone.

"But they are!" Hedge shot back at him.

"*Non, non, non –* "

"I say again, M'sieur, they *are*. You forget that wretched hippie commune in the Ardèche. One should never trust the Americans too far, though I'm not to be quoted on that." Confound the French, Hedge thought with suppressed fury, if a thing's far enough away they sweep it under the carpet of shrugged shoulders. "The man Tex is – "

"Ah, so. Yes. But he is, I think, of little account – "

"You don't mean to say you're not looking for him any more, do you?" Hedge asked belligerently.

"*Non, non,* this I do not mean, M'sieur." The voice was as angry as his own; the cut call clicked in his ear like a French oath. Hedge turned on Roberts-White, venting his frustration. "Really, you'd have imagined one of those passers by would have known Shard was an Englishman at least."

This non sequitur didn't seem worth any response from Roberts-White, who was up to his ears in work and worry. Threats to men in positions of high authority were nothing new, in a personal sense one grew blasé, checked the underside of one's car and hoped for the best. You took other sensible precautions, naturally: you avoided Jewish restaurants when the PLO was feeling aggrieved, Middle Eastern ones when the Israelis were on the rampage, and so on. As for the IRA they could be, and were, everywhere. Always. But this time there was an extra edge. Communist Alliance Transatlantic and the Avengers of St Petersburg looked set for a private war and all manner of nastiness could happen and a whole lot of people could get hurt – and the forthcoming conference was, Roberts-White knew well, vital. It was a pity the FO had sent Hedge; the Embassy's own security men were on the ball and simply didn't need him. And Hedge wasn't easily set aside; he infiltrated himself into everything with a determination not to be disregarded. However, the security machine was moving nicely into gear despite Hedge. Paris had been toothcombed by Counter-Espionage and by the stalwarts of the Police Judicaire aided by the *gendarmerie* made available to the police by the Minister of Defence. Paris was swarming with plain clothes men, extra guards were being placed on the Elysée Palace, the National Assembly, the Palais de Justice, the Hotel de Ville, the Invalides . . . even the Louvre since for a lark the terrorists often liked to slash the odd masterpiece. That, and a lot else. The river wasn't being neglected; frogmen had been down, and would keep on going down, to inspect the great stone supports of the bridges and ensure that no infernal devices were attached to blow as the brass swept across the Seine. Full diving teams, too, had been alerted – army, navy, police. They would go into action at a moment's notice. The Eiffel Tower swarmed with security men with stripped-down automatic rifles concealed about their persons. The Eiffel Tower was a fine vantage point, and not only that, it would make a spectacular set for a bomb. Far-fetched maybe, but the French were an imaginative race whatever else they might or might not be.

★   ★   ★

Shard had answered nothing; the Cossack type – his name had emerged as Nicholas, no surname uttered – seemed unsure of what to do about Shard's silence. He struck Shard as a decent old man, far from being a killer at least in a personal sense. He would cheerfully do what he regarded as his duty, i.e. to

103

assassinate top Communists, but he might well draw the line at slaughtering a defenceless captive, a prisoner-of-war in a sense. The Russians, both Moscow and St Petersburg variety, were bloody enough, and merciless. But old Nicholas had been a long, long time away from Russia – he had been brought up in the milder French environment almost from babyhood, as he had said.

That counted. Nicholas was no bastard. Mikhail was a different kettle of fish. Life had made him so. His face was vicious and his temper vile. Mikhail would stop at nothing, he would show no tender regard for anyone's skin. He stormed about the room and even little fat Annie began to look scared.

He stopped in front of Shard. He had a knife in his hand and this he placed against Shard's throat.

"Talk," he said.

"Sorry. What's the point, anyway? Any efficient terrorist knows the general drill security-wise, has a pretty good idea what he's up against."

"He does not always know the programme. Where the target will be at any given time."

Shard grinned into Mikhail's face. "You have a point. I take it you don't know the relevant movements. I have to say that I don't either."

"You are a liar."

"Right, so I'm a liar if you say so. But there's another thing efficient terrorists know: route and timing changes are endemic to state visits and conferences when terrorism's in the air, right?"

Mikhail scowled, his face ugly.

Shard said, "They don't always confide in me, not right away. Decisions are made and then I get my orders. I'm only a cog in the wheel. Currently I'm a few hours out of date."

Mikhail made a threatening movement with the knife. Old man Nicholas grabbed for his arm, pulled it back from Shard's throat. "Be careful, Mikhail. What he says is true. Remember there are more important things for him . . . please do not forget that, Mikhail."

Mikhail turned his head and met the old Russian's eye. His mouth thinned to a narrow line, but after a few moments he nodded and relaxed. He turned on his heel, called to little fat Annie, and left the room with her. Nicholas with the Kalashnikov was to be the sentry. Shard ran his mind over what had been said. The inference was that these people had some use for him and he had to live, had to be uninjured so as to perform. There, his mind hesitated. He could see, thus far, no way in which he could be used. They'd said he wasn't to be a hostage; that might or might not be the truth – but he could in fact see no likely use for a hostage. Detective Chief Superintendents might not be two a penny, but they didn't have much rank against the pinnacles of the western and eastern Establishments and no-one was going to remit security on their behalf. Shard was expendable and knew it. So too would Nicholas, but not perhaps Mikhail, who had been conditioned to accept the police, Russian variety, as the arbiters of all fate. To Mikhail, Shard might well be the equivalent of the Head of the KGB. If so, a valuable catch.

Nicholas remained silent, just sitting and holding the Kalashnikov. Over his head a clock ticked away on the wall. Time . . . how long before the non-persons and the Avengers of St Petersburg went into the final act?

Shard's thoughts roved on. Asipov, the defected gas expert, dead in London. What had been his idea – had he intended to warn the British of what was planned? No: why should he do that? He was himself one of the Avengers – possibly because of what the Soviets had done to his unacknowledged son. Could be that Asipov had just meant to get out before the balloon went up. Then perhaps he had ideas of taking up his fatherhood somewhere in the west, together perhaps with Ernestine Kolnisenko. Anyway, he was dead now. He could scarcely affect current issues any more.

But there was still a query and an important one. Shard, the non-answerer of questions, asked another of his own – Nicholas hadn't seemed to object earlier. It was a weird situation, Shard thought, for a captive . . .

He said, "You told me Asipov was one of your Avengers,

also that the Russians wanted him back because he was party to your plans."

"Yes."

"Then surely it follows from that, Moscow had got wind of them too, even that Asipov had been made to talk?"

Nicholas nodded and said, "Yes."

"Then why haven't they reacted? And what's the point of your going on with all this?"

Nicholas smiled, almost with a benevolent look. Shard reflected that the old man had probably been much more ferocious in his youth and young manhood. He said, "The Soviet leadership never reacts overtly. It is of course true that they will take extra precautions now. But always leaders expect to be targets for dissidents. It is nothing new. It makes our task the harder, that is all."

"It doesn't affect your confidence?"

"No. Now I shall tell you something else, and perhaps this something will tell you that it would be wise to talk to us." The old man leaned forward, still clutching the Kalashnikov. "It is this. It is surmise but may well become fact. The Soviet delegation will try to turn what we do away from themselves and towards the western leaders – "

"How, for God's sake?"

Again Nicholas smiled. "It can be done. A Russian insistence on those changes in the programme that you spoke of. There will be times when the eastern leaders will be together in one place, the western leaders together somewhere else. We shall try to act against the Soviet persons only, not the others. Moscow will know this. If they engineer a last-minute change of programme so that where the east is supposed to be, the west in fact is . . . I think you follow, yes?"

Shard began to feel something like Nemesis closing in. He said, "Yes, I follow all right."

"Then perhaps you will help us, in the British interest, the safety indeed of all the western leaders."

That was when Shard really began to sweat.

★ ★ ★

Down south in Bourg St Andeal the police had had no luck with the man Frigger, one of the sidekicks to Tex. He had been broken all right, but he didn't know anything helpful that would lead to Tex. Frigger was thick, as thick as his metal ball with its spikes. Just a strong-arm man. He was duly charged with murder of police officers and the report went through to the Police Judicaire in Paris. Paris always thought it knew best and a high-ranking officer was sent south to the Ardèche to put the pressure on Frigger. The result was the same. Nothing. The police chief in Bourg St Andéol was in no way displeased to be able to say I told you so and the high-ranker helicoptered back north in a huff.

Meanwhile Tex was in Paris.

The ten-gallon hat had gone, so had all the gear familiar to the hippies. God had come down to earth in a different sense. Divinity was out. Tex was mortal and wore a light-coloured suit, very smart, that he had bought off the peg in the outskirts of a provincial town whilst en route for Paris. He had travelled north as far as this town in a vegetable lorry, a stowaway beneath the cauliflowers, disembarking when the driver stopped to go into a *pissoir*. Better clad, he had caught a train into Paris and had then walked unremarked to an address in a side street between the Rue du Faubourg St Antoine and the Boulevard Voltaire, where he was welcomed by friends. The friends, two men and a woman, were British with communist links, fellow members in fact of CAT.

While Tex awaited onward transport, a scratch meal was provided, coffee and sandwiches, and money was handed to Tex, a large sum in French francs for expenses and handouts.

"Thanks," Tex said, drinking coffee. He added witheringly, "Bloody hippies."

"Why?"

"Buggered off."

"Yes, we heard." The speaker coughed a lungful of phlegm into a handkerchief, then drew on his Gauloise. "Can't say I blame 'em . . . sodding police."

"Oppressors of the working class," the woman put in violently.

"Sure. Same in the States, same everywhere."

"In Russia it's different."

"Sure, sure."

There was a silence; Tex was resting and just for now there was no special hurry. Let the panic die down, was Tex's philosophy. Suddenly he laughed. "Won't find those fucking UFOs now, not without me."

He was joined in his laughter. Stupid sods, fancy believing . . . but they were mostly from middle class homes, the hippies. Workers had too much to do to keep alive, no time to be hippies – broadly, that was. Tex had specialised in hippies with resources. The more middle class they were, the more gullible, so were their parents who couldn't abide to think of little Johnny without cash in his pocket, no matter what. The UFO idea had been a good one. The woman asked if the scattering of the hippies had mucked up Tex's schedule.

"Jesus," Tex said in brief dismissal. Evidently it hadn't. The woman chewed on a ham sandwich, teeth working as though biting angrily into privilege. When she spoke she had a Glasgow accent, but she wasn't risking it through the ham. She knew more or less the role of the hippies: cover. So long as the cover hadn't been blown, by which she meant so long as Tex himself was in the clear and unsuspected, all was well. No worries. Tex would cope with what he'd come to do. The enemy would be ironed out. That included a man named Hedge. On Tex's arrival, the friends had passed on a report about Hedge, who was said to be in evidence around the British Embassy. "D'you know the man?" the woman had enquired. "Because we don't." Tex said yes, he knew of him. A puffed-up little bastard, could be mistaken for a faggot but wasn't. High up in the British Foreign Office, a big shot. Tex reckoned something could have leaked and that could have accounted for the presence of Hedge in Paris. While eating he did some thinking and as he finished his coffee he reached a decision. He had a job for the Paris cell.

He said, "This Hedge. Plump, not exactly fat. Short. City type clothes – suit, polished shoes, always wears a hat – Derby."

108

"Bowler."

"Okay, bowler. I've seen photographs, ones he won't know were ever taken. Jesus, you can't miss him."

"So?"

"So get him," Tex said briefly. "Fast. Alive. When you've done that take him to House Four, right?"

It was arranged. Later that day a Citroën pulled up outside and a man got out, banged the door, didn't lock it, but lifted a hand to scratch his face when he was in line with the window. A very obvious scratch, which was interpreted to Tex by the Glasgow woman: the awaited transport. Tex took his leave, got into the car, and drove off.

He headed south again, but not far out of Paris. Paris was the hub of future events and time was ticking past.

*   *   *

In London the Foreign Secretary was being given a last-minute briefing, a stiffener really, along with his Minister of State and Permanent Under-Secretary, for the Paris meeting. This was something like the fourth session, since the Prime Minister wished to be very, very sure. Nothing, but nothing, was to be given away. Not an inch. The Prime Minister was Mrs Heffer, no connexion with the Cambridge booksellers. (Mr Heffer was an architect but no longer had designs on Mrs Heffer; he had been divorced, cast aside in the hot pursuit of power.) Margaret Thatcher had set a precedent: Mrs Heffer had determined to follow it. Women Prime Ministers were tougher than men. She was always adamant and knew she was more than a match for the Russians, but her Foreign Secretary was sometimes hesitant and a man, which was why the PM had suddenly decided to go herself. More as an overseer than a participant. Like Hedge, the Foreign Secretary's job was in danger. He was being watched.

Mrs Heffer sat at the head of the table in Number Ten, firm, unyielding.

"You must counter every Russian move, Roly," she said.

"But Prime Minister, the diplomatic – "

"Every Russian move, Roly."

"Yes, Prime Minister. But if I may say so, some resilience often brings – "

"No, Roly."

"But if there's an advantage to be – "

"Ah, an advantage, yes." The PM straightened her back, hefting her breasts up above the table, almost pointing them at the Foreign Secretary, like guns. "But it really has to be an advantage. That's up to you. Under certain circumstances I can *of course* concede a little."

The Foreign Secretary wiped his brow. Number Ten could be a hot place. "Yes, quite, Prime Minister. Quite. I know your views, of course, and they'll be adhered to I promise you. But you see, the French – "

"I'm not concerned with the French," the PM said. "I don't believe they'll give as much trouble as you've been suggesting. They dislike opposing me over EEC matters and this will be the same. I shall be behind you, Roly. I shall *insist* on certain clauses being inserted into any agreement."

"Yes, quite. Yes, indeed. But there's this threat that's been reported from – "

"That's quite a different matter," Mrs Heffer said briskly, "and it doesn't frighten me."

"Of course not, Prime Minister, but do you really think it wise to go to Paris in the changed circumstances?"

The Prime Minister gave a snort and rose from the table. The briefing was at an end. The Foreign Secretary rose like an obedient jack-in-the-box and shuffled his papers back into his brief-case. He looked tired, sad and very worried. It had been a long climb to the Foreign Office by way of Planning and Local Government, Transport, Social Services and the Home Office. And he didn't want to be blown up.

10

Hedge had gone to the Prefecture in person. There was so much to be discussed. He went in an Embassy car and neither he nor the driver noticed the Renault that did an amazing job of tailing, managing to keep always either two or three cars behind. When Hedge got out at the Prefecture, the Renault drove on past and its driver, a man, used his car radio. An unsuspecting Hedge was taken to the Prefect of Police, who remained polite and amiable and somehow managed to disguise his impatience.

Hedge was anxious for ideas on how the terrorists might go into action – *French* ideas which might well be different from those of Roberts-White and the Embassy's security men. "Rocket launchers," he mused. "The IRA use them in Northern Ireland, you know."

"I know, yes. Very, very nasty."

"Well?"

The police chief spread his hands and shrugged magnificently, but said nothing. He considered the suggestion crazy; a Paris summit wasn't the Bogside or whatever. This, when it came, would be found more subtle. Hedge advanced other ideas in the absence of anything from the Prefect. Bombs, gas, guns, planted explosive, time devices, poison-tipped umbrellas. The Prefect nodded at each, agreeing with them all. Each, he said, was likely.

"Some more than others?" Hedge prompted acidly.

"No, no . . ."

"Have you nothing else to suggest?"

The Prefect smiled pacifically. "There is little that is new beneath the sun, M'sieur. Guns and powder, they are the basis."

"Quite. But there's also nuclear weapons."

"Not, I think, on Paris."

"I don't see why not."

"These people, we understand, intend to kill only the Russian delegation. Not all of half of France."

Hedge simmered. What a statement! And how criminally foolish not to take everything into account, even the most fantastic things. You never knew. You had to be ready. It stood to reason. Hedge went on. There was, he said, no end to terrorism's inventiveness; the Prefect was wrong to say there was nothing new. Little nuclear pellets, say: they could be put anywhere. Under tables, in the lavatory cisterns, in bathroom cupboards, disguised as other things, safe things. Poison could be administered by means other than umbrellas. Any member of the many staffs could have been suborned. Hedge waved aside the protestations about rigid screening procedures. Evil persons still slipped through the tightest of nets. Why, they'd even had them in Britain!

The Prefect of Police had had enough. He stood up and thrust out a hand which Hedge was obliged to grasp. He said, "It was so kind of you to come, M'sieur – "

"I've not – "

"I shall tell you what I believe."

"Yes?"

"What is to happen, what method is to be employed . . . this we shall know if and when it happens. Until then, M'sieur, we have no way of knowing. Our efforts must be to prevent anything at all happening, and if we can do this, then all these cogitations will not have been needed."

He smiled, pressed a bell on his desk, a minion came in and Hedge was escorted out, by this time speechless beyond a muttered goodbye. All this trouble, all this humiliation, and for what? For the Russians, people who were beneath contempt! Hedge didn't give a pin for the safety of the Russians *per se*. Russians were just a confounded nuisance, frankly better dead. But of course there was the British delegation – and the PM. He must as it were set his sights on her. As he had reflected once before, it wasn't always only the target that got hit. If only the French police would pull their wretched fingers out. Meanwhile they provided Hedge with transport back to the British Embassy. Once again the Renault wasn't noticed. Nor, when Hedge reached the Faubourg St Honoré, was the woman in the least noticeable. Glasgow-drab, she mingled with the shadows and kept her eyes open. The Renault went past, its driver once again using his two-way radio. While Hedge remained in the Embassy, the Renault was relieved by a Simca, which took up its station in a side street within range of a small transistorised transceiver concealed between the woman's breasts, uncomfortably but safely. It was not long before Hedge came out again. This time he was on foot; he didn't want cars that might be known for Embassy ones approaching the Hotel Aviatic. He preferred to use the Metro, anonymously. He did, with the woman behind him. He descended at Concorde, whence he could go straight through to Montparnasse-Bienvenue, about the same distance from the Hotel Aviatic as was Saint-Placide.

As Hedge went down the steps, the woman spoke briefly into her corsage. Thereafter she travelled in the same carriage as Hedge. From Montparnasse she tailed him to his hotel, then once again used her communication system. Her call was picked up in the Simca, which at once left its side street off the Faubourg St Honoré and drove fast for the Rue de Vaugirard. Two men got out, one of them tall and hefty with a face like granite, the other weasely but dangerous-looking.

They went into the Hotel Aviatic and the hefty one asked for Mr Hedge. Yes, he was in.

"What room?"

"I am sorry, I cannot – I will telephone for him to come down – "

"No. Room number, please. British police officers, from Scotland Yard." Briefly, well palmed, a nondescript card was flashed. The room number was given and the men went up in the lift. As the big man knocked on Hedge's door he heard, faintly, the simultaneous ring of a telephone – a warning, from Reception. Inside, Hedge dithered then chose wrong. Leaving the telephone to ring unanswered meanwhile, he went to the door. The moment he opened it, the men moved. Handcuffs were snapped around Hedge's wrists and he felt the hard ring of metal that pressed into his side.

"What – what – "

"Shut up," the man said. The smaller man deftly wound a heavy gag around Hedge's mouth and chin and he was propelled along to the lift and then down to the entrance lobby. The girl in Reception, joined now by a young man, stared at gagged Hedge, at his captors.

"Obscene language," the big man said. "Not for young ladies."

Without delay or interference Hedge was marched out into the street, feet twinkling in an effort to keep up with himself, and bundled into the Simca.

*   *   *

Shard had responded to the old Russian's suggestion that in the West's interest he might find it possible to tell what he knew: he could not, he said, do that. His job was, had to be, in the Russian interest also. Neither Britain, nor France, nor any other EEC country, could countenance the assassination of persons who were party to the conference.

"Then you place at risk your own people."

"Perhaps. I'm still not talking. Not that I have much to talk about."

The old man regarded him silently. His fingers shook a little on the Kalashnikov. It wasn't a reassuring sight. In the air was a hint of Shard being inadvertantly colandered. He was considering this when Mikhail came back into the room. He spoke in Russian to the old man, staring at Shard as he did so. Shard caught the name of the Soviet Foreign Minister, A.Y. Hokadian. Neither Mikhail nor Nicholas gave him a translation, but Mikhail said to him in English, "Now the time is close and we shall move."

No more than that; Mikhail left the room again. From somewhere outside Shard heard little fat Annie singing. It sounded like a happy song though Russian. Love, perhaps.

114

Shard wondered if the girl was still thinking of Tex or had shifted her whole allegiance to Mikhail. Presumably, since she was happy, the latter. Little fat Annie was an intellectual desert, happy merely to be with a man and never mind what that man intended to do to world peace. That obtuseness just could be worth bearing in mind. Dumb girls could be manipulated. Perhaps. Perhaps not; sometimes they had a strong streak of obstinacy. Their very dumbness wrapped them in a cocoon. The singing came nearer and the girl came into the room, smiling, doing a little happy dance like a baby elephant. Old Nicholas regarded her indulgently, like a father. Or in his case a grandfather. The whole scene struck Shard as immensely weird; the Kalashnikov didn't fit. The happy, inconsequential fat girl and the old man, with the fires of youth damped down into geriatricism, softened almost into a kind of benevolence, didn't seem part of the assassination plot at all. Yet, oddly, Shard still had the idea that Nicholas was in charge rather than Mikhail.

Little fat Annie grinned at Shard. "Hullo," she said.

"Hullo, Annie. You sound happy."

"I am," she said. He saw she had made a daisy chain and had put it round her neck. A country girl at heart, and never mind the grimness of her home town of Kharkov in the coalfields of the Ukraine? Certainly the hippie field in the Ardèche had appeared to suit her.

She approached Nicholas, singing again. She took the daisy chain from her neck. "For you," she said. "Bend your head." The old man did so; Annie lifted the daisy chain. The Kalashnikov swung a little sideways. Shard sweated, felt the pounding of his heart. He had been straining at the ropes on his wrists; there was a little play . . . if only there had been just a little more. The moment passed when footsteps were heard approaching and Mikhail came into the room. He spoke in Russian and went out again. The old man ordered Shard to his feet and moved behind him with the Kalashnikov prodding into his back. In the integral garage the Dormobile was waiting. Shard was put back into the toilet compartment and the vehicle, with Nicholas and the

girl in the passenger seats and Mikhail at the wheel, was
backed out.

★   ★   ★

"I don't know what you imagine you're doing," Hedge panted
in the back of the Simca. He was free of the gag and doing his
best to maintain his dignity. "Do you know who I am?"

"Yes," the big man said.

"Then you'll – "

"Shut up."

"I beg your pardon?"

"Granted. Now shut up, Hedge."

Hedge gave a gasp. They *did* know! What, for God's sake,
had happened to security? And what was to happen to the PM
and the Foreign Secretary – for that matter, to himself,
which was a much more immediate thought. He looked sideways; the small man was alongside him and there was a
revolver thrust into his ribs and something about the look in
the small man's eye told him that the revolver would be used if
necessary and never mind the fact of the busy Paris streets.
The thing was silenced, he could tell that from the size and
feel of the part that was pressing into him. There would be a
phut and that would be all. Probably they wouldn't kill him,
he wouldn't have been kidnapped if he hadn't had value to
them, but he would be wounded and might bleed to death if
there were any traffic hold-ups. Or he might be shot in the
knee-cap, like the IRA did in Belfast. Hedge trembled and felt
sweat run stickily. What a damnable situation. He couldn't
imagine what might be wanted of him. The whole idea of
kidnapping him was so inept. There would be consternation in
the Embassy, indeed in Whitehall – these people might have
known there would be a real toothcomb drawn through Paris,
on orders from the very top. Not only Paris; all France. Then
Hedge's heart sank: there were so many blasted idiots around
these days, the wrong sort had achieved responsibility and
were unequal to it. That man Roberts-White had referred to
balls-ups and though Hedge still didn't like the term he had
to confess its relevance. Dunderheads abounded and wrong

116

decisions would be made to the detriment, most likely, of his own safety. Roberts-White himself was no great shakes. And some fool in the Foreign Office itself had been responsible for sending the obviously false information that Stanislav Asipov, who seemed to have started all this, had been considered a mere plant for future use by the Soviet intelligence services . . .

"Sheer twaddle!" Hedge said aloud.

"What is?" the big man asked from the front.

"Oh, nothing."

"Shut up, then."

Hedge relapsed into silence. The voice had held a definite threat. The Simca seemed to fly through the traffic, missing other cars by centimetres, just managing to pull up in time at pedestrian crossings. In no time at all Hedge was utterly lost; they had entered parts of Paris that Hedge had never been in and would never have wanted to be in. Something that looked rather like London's East End. Warehouses, factories, rows of horrible little dwellings, and soon a stench of Seine. Not a salubrious part. If Paris had been closer to the river's mouth this would probably have been dockland. As it was, it was nondescript; the only vessels were small ones, barges mostly, and here and there a vessel fitted with passenger seats on the upper deck, river pleasure craft undergoing refit.

As the Simca stopped at one of the nasty little houses, close to some derelict premises that ran down to the river, Hedge felt extremely uneasy. Bodies could be disposed of in rivers, no trouble at all – weighted sacks came into his mind, or the holds of barges. A concrete slab with a man embedded in it would sink quickly, never to rise again. Or he could form a part of the foundations of a by-pass.

Hedge was ordered out and, between the two men, was shepherded into the house, which smelt of cooking oil, garlic and the emanations of the river.

The river!

Hedge remembered something: the programme for the VIPs had included two excursions on the Seine, one of them an afternoon trip laid on for the Russian delegation at their special request, the other a real show-off to all the VIPs, Paris by night, a dinner party aboard a *bateau mouche* . . .

There could be a connexion, perhaps.

If so then he, Hedge, might be at the heart of it. To win or lose it all: that was quite a thought, and a worrying one.

★   ★   ★

The report went in to the house between the Rue du Faubourg St Antoine and the Boulevard Voltaire, being conveyed by a leather-clad motor-cyclist: House Four, safe arrival. The woman from Glasgow received it, then used the telephone. Tex hadn't arrived at his destination yet, but would be informed as soon as he did so. The motor-cyclist left, with orders to hold the captive incommunicado and alive. House Four would be informed when Hedge was required to be produced. It wouldn't be long now.

When the motor-cyclist got back to House Four, Hedge had been securely locked into a basement. It was very damp from its proximity to the river, and it smelt foul. The very air was foetid. It was totally dark. Hedge sank into a trembling heap of misery on a cold, damp stone floor. At first there had been some euphoria about being at the heart of things – stupid, really, when as a prisoner there was nothing useful he could do, but it had been there along with thoughts of a visit to Buckingham Palace afterwards – but by now it had gone. For one thing, Hedge so far had no idea which of the two factions had kidnapped him. The Avengers of St Petersburg, the non-persons – or the man Tex from the hippie commune? If it was the non-persons, then he really could be at the heart. If it was Tex and the wretched Communist Alliance Transatlantic, then equally he could be near the heart, since the man Tex was anxious to get his hands on non-person Mikhail Asipov. Or was said to be. Thus, where Mikhail was, or where Mikhail was perhaps expected to be, then so also could be Tex. That stood to reason. Conversely, where Tex was, then Mikhail might be expected. At any rate, somewhere in the vicinity.

Suppose the non-persons, the undead, intended to prove, in this vicinity, their fact of living – prove it here, on the

118

Seine, when the VIPs embarked? Suppose Tex and CAT knew that?

Hedge gave a pathetic moan. What was the use of conjecture? He was powerless to act upon it; if he managed to piece together a hypothesis, it would be no more, really, than being wise after the event. He couldn't communicate it. If he could communicate, damn it all, he'd communicate his whereabouts and be rescued by a determined squad from the GIGN! That thought led him back to Shard. Where was Shard, who if he was free would naturally have pulled out every possible stop to get his chief back to safety?

*   *   *

"Gone," Roberts-White said briefly to Eve Brett. "Hooked away from his hotel by a subterfuge. Not very bright of him."

"What do we do, sir?"

"Refer it to HE," the First Secretary said. He left the room after contacting his immediate chief, a counsellor. One did not approach the Ambassador direct, nor use the telephone to him except in dire emergency. Counsellor and First Secretary went together for an audience of HE.

The Ambassador was concerned. "Shard, and now Hedge. Damn! It seems this thing's for real, not that I ever doubted that. Do we react, or don't we, that's the first question." He drummed his fingers on his desk. Neither the Counsellor nor Roberts-White offered an opinion; such had not precisely been asked for. The Ambassador answered his own query. "I shall of course inform Whitehall and the Elysée Palace . . . but as for Hedge himself, we play him down. I've a feeling whoever's got him has an inflated idea of his importance in the scheme of things. At this stage we don't want to appear rattled by his loss." He looked up with an impish look in his eye. "*Does* Hedge rattle?"

He was looking at Roberts-White, who took the point and said, "No, sir."

"Not much actual use?"

"I'm afraid not, sir. I hope that doesn't sound disloyal."

"Never mind disloyalty, Roberts-White, always be *honest*."

119

"Yes, sir."

"And his knowledge of the plans is certainly no more than mine and that's little enough currently."

"Sir?" The Counsellor raised an eyebrow.

"Changes," the Ambassador said briefly. "The French are worried and I'm far from surprised. They're proposing changes in the programme – I don't know the details yet. It's all in the melting pot."

"Is there any suggestion of a cancellation?" the Counsellor asked.

"No. But that's exactly what I'm going to put to Whitehall, now this has happened." The Ambassador made a gesture of dismissal. "I'll let you know the result."

★ ★ ★

His Excellency's submission cut no ice at all. The Elysée Palace considered that matters had already gone too far, that a cancellation would almost certainly be misconstrued in Moscow, even if deliberately, and the NATO military brass would be furious at cold feet. But, as a result of Embassy pressure, the French President made contact by telephone with Downing Street, speaking personally to the Prime Minister.

"Good gracious, no!" Mrs Heffer said. "As I've already told Henry," she went on in reference to Her Majesty's Ambassador, "*I'm* certainly not going to back down. No, no, the conference goes ahead just as planned so far as I'm concerned." She paused. "Of course, if you're frightened by the possible consequences . . . it *is* your country, after all."

She managed to sound as though she was doubtful about even that proposition. The President, caught on a raw nerve by the suggestion of fright, backed down. "*Non, non, Madame. Je ne –* "

"That's all right, then," Mrs Heffer said. After a little polite conversation, she rang off. She turned to the Foreign Secretary. "The French are always co-operative if handled right, Roly. And this conference *must* go ahead and Moscow put in its place – I can't consider delay. You know – they're such *frightful* people."

"The French, Prime Minister?"

"The *Russians*, Roly."

In Paris the President thought it only proper to call Moscow and never mind the British intransigence; Moscow had been kept informed as to the threat, naturally, and might react to the new development. But they did not. The reply came very positively from the Kremlin: "*Niet.*"

Next day, two things happened: in Paris there was a conference between the Elysée Palace, the Prefecture, the GIGN, the Defence Ministry and the Embassies of all countries party to the main summit for which the delegations would arrive the following day; and in London Mrs Heffer left for the north to brief the Queen, on holiday at Balmoral, on all affairs to be discussed in Paris. Despite the holiday atmosphere of informality, the Prime Minister was met by a royal car and a prince at Dyce airport and at Balmoral by a pipe band found by the Argyll and Sutherland Highlanders, a wish of Mrs Heffer's that had been discreetly made known in advance of her arrival. As she reported to Roly on her return that same evening, the Queen had been charming, a very good listener as always, no interruptions. She had expressed concern for the missing men, Hedge and Shard; and had been informed by the Prime Minister that their safety would of course be a main consideration.

"Not the *only* one I need hardly say. The Queen was worried about this wretched threat, of course. As I said to you yesterday, Roly, the Russians are such frightful people. I told her that."

"Did she agree, Prime Minister?"

"Not agree, Roly. She couldn't, in her position. I instanced those stories that reached us some time ago – the fact that the Russians had used *slave labour* on the Siberian end of that pipeline – the gas. Men, women and children, even the sick, brought in from the prison encampments, working under armed guards and whips – *terrible*. We *simply must* have this conference, I told her and deflect the French from *too much détente* . . . in my opinion, I said, *ultimate peace* depends on our efforts *now* . . ."

The Prime Minister crossed the room and looked into a

mirror, critically. She had had an appointment with her hair-dresser the day before; she would have preferred today, but there had been Balmoral. *Chic*, elegance, femininity were much admired in Paris, which was in so many ways more civilised than today's London, and Margaret Thatcher had always been absolutely impeccable. Mrs Heffer pushed a little at her hair, sighed, and went back to her desk. There was so much to do. What a nuisance people were who went and got kidnapped. She had entirely agreed with the Ambassador's advice that the man Hedge be played down.

Across the channel there had been a good deal of dissension as the parties, so hastily and unexpectedly summoned together by the President, got down to business. A change in the prog-ramme, as suggested by the Ambassador, was the principal subject. But all places of assembly could be equally dangerous and no security was one hundred per cent watertight, as the man from the GIGN insisted, waving his arms in the air and sometimes closing his eyes as he made an emotional point. Yes, some changes, by all means, such was only prudent, but no, he would not commit himself between one suggestion and another. Each had its good and bad points. But one thing stood out to all present: the purely pleasure aspects should be curtailed if not cancelled altogether. The GIGN chief himself made this point firmly; the President agreed. Number One danger might be the two trips on the river.

"The frogmen, the diving teams, they cannot be every-where at once. It is too dangerous in my view."

The river excursions were cancelled. Something else could be substituted, but what? To take the delegates to the top of the Eiffel Tower would be lunacy. Besides, most of them could be presumed to have done it before. The river trips had been intended to be different, a pleasant way, if the weather held, of combining a leisurely view of Paris with informal inter-delegation talks on a friendly basis. The President was especially sad to cancel his own idea, the jolly notion of the splendid dinner to be held aboard two *bateaux mouches*, good food and wine and Paris by night. Even the Russians showed obvious regret when that jaunt was veto-ed; it didn't show in their granite faces, but there was a hint that they'd been thinking that soft fairy lights, and old stone bridges glimpsed as shadows in the night, and excellent food, and very much good French wine, and brandy, might have induced the French to be even more reasonable in the unofficial give-and-take.

In the end, after a submission from the British Ambassador that whatever was decided upon it would be very advisable to keep the east and west delegations entirely separate when not in conference – because the threat was specific to the Russians, and he didn't want to incur the opprobrium of letting the Prime Minister be inadvertently blown up, though he didn't exactly mention this aspect – a decision was reached that no informal festivities at all would be laid on. Just the inescapable official parades, guard inspections and welcomes and so on, nothing that could offer a target unnecessarily.

"No fun?" the American NATO representative asked.

"*Non.*" This was the French President, and he was firm. But he had failed to reckon on Mrs Heffer.

11

The Dormobile had been driven a long way; for Shard it was an uncomfortable time. The driving was very fast and the vehicle swayed badly on bends. When at last it stopped and Shard was brought out the day had long gone, but in the darkness the sheen of water could still be seen. In the distance something tall loomed; it could be a cathedral. But the immediate surroundings were of less note. Just some sheds of corrugated iron, like wartime Nissen huts, on a river bank.

The Dormobile was run into a garage and Shard was taken under guard of old Nicholas with the Kalashnikov into one of the huts. Mikhail shone a torch into darkness. The light showed up a pile of junk in one corner – sacks, old crates and packing cases. Mikhail kicked some of the clutter aside; a trapdoor showed. He bent and lifted it, shone the torch down. There was a ladder. Shard was helped down this in front of the Kalashnikov. In the torch beam as Mikhail followed Nicholas down with little fat Annie Shard saw three men sitting on a long bench, each of them with an automatic rifle, each rifle fitted with telescopic sights. The men had the same look as Mikhail – cadaverous men with haunted eyes, watchful eyes, and a strange look of withdrawal as though they were unused to normal company – the look of the non-persons, the undead? Shard's eye took in boxes filled with grenades and other explosives, plus ammunition for the rifles.

"All eventualities covered," he said.

"All eventualities."

"In other words, the plan's not yet finalised."

There was no answer from Mikhail. He nodded at the old man, and Shard was pushed forward by the Kalashnikov to sit on the bench. His hands were still tied behind his back, but during the long ride in the Dormobile he had managed to loosen the ropes further. Mikhail spoke in Russian to the armed zombies and received monosyllabic answers. After that there was a curious stillness, a silence broken only by a faint slop of water. Before entering the hut Shard had seen the dark outline of a river barge alongside a ramshackle jetty, and there had been something of a wind. The sounds would be the slop of small waves against the side of the barge. Sitting on the bench, Shard waited for more questioning; but it did not come. Curiouser and curiouser. Mikhail had gone back up the ladder. Little fat Annie had curled up on the bare floor like a cat, and had gone to sleep.

*　　　*　　　*

"There's been a contact," Roberts-White reported to the Counsellor. "Hedge."

"Don't say he's back?"

Roberts-White smiled. "No. The men who've got him – they've been in touch. It appears he's in the hands of CAT."

"And?"

"He's being held as a kind of security, a long-stop if you like. They think they've got hold of a crock of gold – "

"That's what HE feared, isn't it?"

"Yes," Roberts-White said, "but I don't think it matters all that much. Except perhaps to Hedge . . . Because of his supposed importance, CAT is putting the pressure on."

The Counsellor was showing signs of impatience. "Oh, come *on*. Just tell me what they said."

"Right. CAT doesn't want any changes in the VIP programme. Any changes and Hedge has had it."

The Counsellor stared thoughtfully. "You mean they'll kill him?"

"That seems to be the idea."

"But *why*, for heaven's sake? Didn't you say this man Tex was after Mikhail Asipov, not the – "

"That's right. And the best way for CAT to bowl out the Avengers of St Petersburg is for CAT to know just where to find Mikhail and his non-persons. Or anyway, to have a pretty

125

good general idea where they're likely to strike, which will obviously be somewhere along the line of the agreed programme. And you see, if there are changes . . . well, those changes might remain a closed book to Mikhail and his associates."

The Counsellor blew out his cheeks. "In which case the VIPs are safe. So what's CAT griping about?"

Roberts-White shrugged. "A question of kudos. Quite apart from the personal Tex/Mikhail angle . . . CAT wants the glory of having saved a bunch of Russians. At least, that's my view."

"What a bloody mess," the Counsellor said, groaning. "It looks like a straight choice, doesn't it?"

"Hedge or the Russian bigwigs. Yes. I'm glad it's not my choice."

"Nor mine either," the Counsellor said promptly. "I'll see what HE says about it . . ."

      ★   ★   ★

Food and water had been taken down to the cellar. A man with an old-world candle lantern had opened up a heavy iron-bound door and come down the stone steps, illuminating Hedge sitting in slime on the stone floor with his knees drawn up, looking the picture of misery and abandonment.

His visitor was French but spoke English. He said, "Eat and drink, M'sieur." He laid down a dish and a jug. On the dish was a filthy mess of smelly meat, some sort of green vegetable, and a potato. Hedge retched; he had no appetite even for good food at the moment.

"I can't possibly eat that," he said in a high voice.

"I shall therefore leave it," the man said. "It will be hard to eat and drink in darkness but the fault is yours."

"Do what you like," Hedge said. The man shrugged and started back up the steps. Hedge whinnied after him, "What's going to happen to me?"

The man stopped, turned, and gave a laugh. "You wish to know, M'sieur?"

"Yes!"

The man told him. Possible death. Hedge gave a gasp of

terror. The man turned away again and went through the door, banging it behind him and sliding the bolts across. In the darkness, Hedge shook and felt fresh sweat start. Hedge he might be, Hedge of the Foreign Office, but he was no international figure, no wars would be started on his account. With the Soviet Foreign Minister and a brace or so of Deputy Premiers in the other side of the balance, hope would be a useless thing to have.

*   *   *

The Ambassador was in a quandary. Hedge could scarcely be left to his fate; for the British to lose a highly-placed Foreign Office official could be serious. And highly-placed was in certain of its aspects not too much of an over-statement: Hedge did after all have the rank and standing of an assistant under-secretary of state. It was in his personality that he was of not much account, and you couldn't hang a man, as it were, merely because he was a tiresome bore. But all this, coming as it had on the heels, or to be more precise slightly in advance, of the arrival of the Whitehall contingent in Paris was a confounded nuisance . . .

"And potentially very dangerous," he said to the Counsellor.

"Very."

"I can't act on my own, that's obvious."

The Counsellor raised an eyebrow. "The Elysée Palace, Your Excellency?"

"Time is short. And the President's unlikely to agree, I imagine. What then?"

The response was pat: "Refer to Whitehall."

The Ambassador gave him a sharp look; there had been a kind of smugness in the tone, a sort of I-know-what-you'll-do-next inference, which was unfair, because all ambassadors always referred everything to Whitehall. Just a message pad, the Ambassador thought moodily, that's all I am . . . he lost no time in calling Whitehall on the security line, deciding to do this in advance of waiting upon the French President so that, as he said, he knew where he stood. He spoke to a deputy

127

under-secretary of state, who immediately got onto Heathrow and caught the Prime Minister in the nick of time before she went with her retinue from the VIP lounge to the waiting jet. Then he rang the Ambassador back. The answer was straight from Mrs Heffer's mouth: no British subject would be sacrificed to the Russians.

"Was that all?" the Ambassador asked.

"Yes, Ambassador."

"Has she considered the matter fully, considered the implications?"

The Deputy Under-Secretary was cautious. "In my opinion possibly not. There was scarcely time." There was a pause. "She'd mislaid her handbag . . . she was preoccupied. Very natural."

"Natural!" the Ambassador repeated bitterly. Lives could hang upon a Prime Minister's handbag. He cut the call, little the wiser as to what he should do. Dig out Hedge from captivity? A likely prospect in the time available! Ask through the proper channels for an urgent audience of the President of France? No time for that either: the Ambassador reached a difficult decision: to hell with protocol.

He used the telephone.

The President was incredulous. *Non*, he would not change his mind. *Non*, the programme would not be restored at the demand of a terrorist. What had the British come to, that they should ask such a thing? He rang off angrily and the bang seemed to go right into the Ambassador's head.

"Now what?" the Counsellor asked.

The Ambassador spread his arms in despair. Mrs Heffer . . . a clash seemed only too likely. He said, "We must be *very* tactful."

*   *   *

Daylight had filtered into the hut, down through the now open trapdoor. None of the non-persons appeared to have slept; perhaps that was why they looked like the undead . . . only little fat Annie had slept right through the night. Now she woke, got up, grinned across at Shard, and went up the ladder. There was no sign of Mikhail. There were sounds coming from the river as barges moved past. Shard's guess, and it was no more than that, was that the river was the Seine, the barges were coming up from Le Havre towards Paris and beyond. The cathedral that he believed he'd seen the night before could have been Rouen.

The knowledge didn't appear to be of much practical use.

Shard looked at the non-persons, the executioners. He wondered where the arms and explosives had come from: old Nicholas, the arranger? But there were always avenues for terrorists, always some arms dealer ready to make money. No sentiment, no loyalties. Cash was the god now. What were the roles of these hopeless-looking men to be? Stationed at strategic intervals along the route of one of the motorcades, peering through their telescopic sights from windows, roofs and suchlike? One at least was bound to get a good opening. No security was hot enough to cover all points even though all buildings from which a threat might be presumed to come would have been checked out, all names known, passes required and examined. Shard had often wondered why there hadn't been more assassinations on formal occasions. A fanatic who didn't mind being caught once he had done his deed would always stand virtually a hundred per cent chance of success. These undead didn't look as though they had anything to live on for. They looked the fanatic part.

After some time had passed Shard heard a car draw up. A door banged, and voices came. Then silence again. The sun was climbing. This was the day of the arrival of the British team: during the afternoon, Mrs Heffer would alight on French soil. The Russians were due in an hour later, four p.m. French time. Not long. Unless a quick dash to Paris was envisaged, it began to seem unlikely that Mikhail meant to strike along the arrival route from the airport.

The car was heard to leave; Mikhail came down the ladder with two other men, men in jeans and donkey jackets, Frenchmen, tough-looking, both of them dark visaged. Mikhail said, "Now we leave." He said something further in Russian; the non-persons got to their feet and climbed the ladder, carrying their rifles, their faces expressionless still. Shard was ordered to get up and follow; he went out with Nicholas behind him as before. The old man hadn't slept so far as Shard knew, remaining on guard throughout the night, as wakeful as the undead, but he had allowed Shard to nod off with his back slumped against the wall.

Outside, the undead were going aboard the barge. Paris was presumably the destination; Shard had no idea how long it would take for them to make the river journey. It still seemed unlikely that the shooting or whatever would come during that first drive into the city.

Once aboard, they all went below. It was a tight fit in the cabin. Shard sat next to little fat Annie, still a happy girl, looking forward to something. The two men who had come in by car remained on deck – the crew. Before embarking they had brought the cases of ammunition and explosives aboard. Within minutes of the embarkation, the barge moved off the jetty under its engine power, chugging along slowly. From the cabin ports Shard could see the countryside going past. Green fields, cows, a scene of peace. From time to time houses and roads and people passing in cars, looking at the barge's progress, none knowing what it contained, what its cargo was, what the concealed men intended, what trouble would be brought to Paris and the whole of the west if they should succeed.

If only he could contact one of them. But probably no-one would believe him.

Time passed. Little fat Annie slept again, slumped against Shard. She breathed heavily without actually snoring. It was like a steam-whistle. Her breasts heaved against him with each intake. At last old Nicholas had gone to sleep and guard duties had been taken over by Mikhail himself.

There had been no more questioning. Shard wondered why. It was possible Mikhail had informers within Paris, men planted, men with big ears. Possible but not likely: Mikhail was a recent import from the Soviet Union, a man without local contacts. Nicholas, on the other hand, had spent his life in France. Any contacts could be his. But if there was an availability of information what did they want with him, Shard?

Mystery abounded. They drew closer to Paris. Or so Shard presumed.

★   ★   ★

The jet from Heathrow came in on schedule, all glitter and airline colours, freshly painted. BRITISH it flaunted. The welcoming committee, the brass both political and military, was nervy. The French Premier hadn't come; Mrs Heffer thought that rude. He was represented by the Foreign Minister, a bouncy, brisk little man with a paunch and an oversmart lounge suit in beige. There was a general and an admiral and the Prefect of Police of Paris, a number of hangers-on, aides and so forth, and there was a guard and band in full dress uniforms. Bayonets glittered in a strong but declining sun and there was the inevitable dog who ran hither and thither and barked loudly when Mrs Heffer appeared at the head of the gangway and waved a hand. The dog was fielded by a military policeman and Mrs Heffer, very British, came down the steps, smiling, a smile straight from a bandbox, blue-rinsed hair, neat coat and skirt in powder blue to match, white silk scarf at the throat, red wash-leather gloves.

She was greeted by the Foreign Minister, who bowed. "So nice to be in France," she said. She shook his hand warmly. He hovered, uncertain whether or not to kiss: the smile was still there but had suddenly turned icy as her eye caught that of a minister from the Embassy.

"No ambassador," she said. "May one ask why that is, Sir Sidney?"

The Minister coughed, dithered. He said, "His Excellency sends his profound apologies, Prime Minister. The telephone call, you remember – "

"Oh, yes. I stated my point of view. I trust it has been conveyed to President Ligot."

"I believe it has, Prime Minister." Sir Sidney seemed nervous.

Mrs Heffer assumed the Ambassador's absence meant he

131

was dealing with the matter. She turned her attention to the waiting French officials. She inspected the guard, rather perfunctorily. Not quite like Her Majesty's Brigade of Guards. Then, accompanied by the Foreign Minister of France, she got into the leading car of a long motorcade drawn up by the airport buildings. She was whisked away fast. No chances. Those left behind breathed a sigh of relief. There was always a likelihood of other brands of terrorism lurking, it wasn't just the Russians who had to be protected, but at least if Mrs Heffer was shot from now on it wouldn't be an airport responsibility.

And now it had all begun, the terrible three days during which Paris would be the focus of the world's attention. Soon all the others would come in. The Russians, the Germans, many others too. Also the everlasting holidaymakers who would get in the way of airport security and if anything happened might go and get caught in the crossfire. More trouble for harassed authorities, but then there was always something even if only a hijack.

In the meantime, unknown to all but a few in Paris, the barge from near Rouen was slowly closing on the capital. And elsewhere Hedge, who had still not eaten despite further offers of inedible foodstuffs, was receiving an important visitor.

12

There had also been a visitor to the barge, a man wearing bright blue crimplene trousers and a yellow T-shirt with stripes, pedalling a bicycle fast from the direction of Paris. The road where he met the barge ran close to the river bank.

He hailed the crew member standing at the helm, a long iron bar projecting from the rudder-head. He wished, he said, to come aboard. He gave what acted as a password and the helmsman brought the barge towards the bank. Nimbly, the cyclist jumped across, landing on the canvas-covered cargo hatch. Going aft, he ducked into the cabin. He was met by Mikhail. They spoke in French.

"What is it, Jacques?"

"A change in the programme. No longer the river."

There was an oath from Mikhail. Shard saw the anger in the face. "Who has told you this?"

"Henri," the cyclist answered. "Henri is very certain. The man Hedge, he has been seized . . . the security is much alarmed by his disappearance and because of this there will be more tightness, according to Henri. So there will be no river voyages."

"And who has seized this Hedge?"

The cyclist shrugged; this, Henri had not known. To Mikhail it was obvious: CAT. He said something brief in Russian. His expression was grim; Shard fancied he was about to strike the cyclist; no bringer of bad tidings was ever welcome. But Mikhail restrained himself as old Nicholas got to his feet and moved across. The old man laid a hand on Mikhail's arm.

"It is done, Mikhail," he said peaceably. "You and I, we

cannot alter that. We must use the alternative now. It was always a possibility that the alternative would – "

"Yes." Mikhail flung the old Russian's arm aside. "Yes, very well, we must do this, I agree. It'll be more dangerous – "

"But we shall still succeed, Mikhail."

This conversation had been in Russian; Shard had not been able to follow much of it. He had been rattled by the news of Hedge. Hedge in captivity could be lethal. Shard believed Hedge hadn't a very high resistance threshold and if he knew anything worth knowing in the current situation he would probably not hold back for long. And what did CAT want him for? Just to garner information, most likely. Shard's mind disconnected from Hedge's plight when Mikhail, after a further discussion with the old man, spoke again to the messenger from Paris. The man was told to return to Paris pronto. He was to give the word to someone called Stolnik: Shard registered the name. Stolnik was to be told that the alternative plan was to be put into operation. Mikhail would be at the rendezvous soon after dark, and Stolnik was to be there with transport for the explosives.

The messenger left the cabin, followed as far as the door by Mikhail. Through the port Shard saw him pedal away fast. The engine started up again and the barge moved off the bank. Mikhail turned back into the cabin; there was a nasty look in his eyes, a vicious look. He didn't like alterations of plan. This was to be the very devil. But he, too, like the French President earlier, had failed to take Mrs Heffer into account.

*   *   *

Hedge's visitor had been the American, Tex. Coming down the steps into the cellar accompanied by the man with the candle-lantern, he stared contemptuously at cringe.

He said, "Well now, Big Shot."

"Who are you?" Hedge asked, though in the circumstances the American accent had been the give-away and he knew he was in the hands of CAT.

"Never mind that. I know who you are. That's all that matters, right? And you're in the know."

"What about?"

"What about? Don't act dumb, Hedge. It doesn't pay, you know that?"

Hedge swallowed, sweated – it ran like rivers down his neck, soaking collar and shirt. His teeth chattered; he couldn't keep them still. He said, "Of course I know about the conference, that's obvious."

"Sure. It's why you're in Paris. Why you're here, too. I want to know something different, right?" Tex approached closer, squatted on his haunches, staring into Hedge's face. "Lard," he said. "Dough. Too much fat. Reckon you may lose some of that, Big Shot. You know something?"

"No . . ."

Tex grinned at him. "This here's an old part of Paris. There's a lot of cellars like this one. Next door, there's an old-time contraption. Brought from the Bastille or some place. An old Frog prison, anyway. They call it a treadmill. Jeez, you'll sweat, Big Shot."

Hedge's mouth opened and shut again. Fear struck; this man was a demon. He thought about his heart. He'd often been bothered about it. His doctor had said it was as sound as a bell but Hedge didn't believe him, and treadmills hadn't been mentioned during the consultation. Now, the heart was beating fast.

Tex, still squatting, said, "What I want to know is about these Avengers of St Petersburg, right? Want to know all about them . . . what *you* know, that is. And don't tell me your British Embassy doesn't know about them. Right?"

"We know about them," Hedge said, his voice squeaking. It could scarcely be denied; he wasn't giving away secrets.

"And what they mean to do. Here in Paris."

"Yes. That, too. Nothing else, though."

"*Nothing* else? You sure, Hedge, dead sure?"

That heart. "Yes!"

"Like what their work-out's going to be?"

"Of course we don't know that! If we did, well, the whole thing would be simple. Surely you see that?"

"I see that, sure. But it doesn't tell me you don't know and

135

that it *will* all be simple like you say. I just want to know, that's all, right?"

"I – I don't know anything."

"Not even when you know about the treadmill, Hedge?"

"No. You can't do that to me! I have a dickey heart." He explained the Anglicism. "A *weak* heart."

"Sure you have. For now, just for now, we'll forget the work-out. There's something else, and this you sure do know. Tell me what the counter-measures are, right? All the details. What's being guarded, what isn't. Strength of police and that – you know what I want."

Hedge did; he also knew why. Shard had established that CAT was out to kill Mikhail Asipov. Tex wanted to know the security set-up, the places and times considered most at risk, just so he could get a line on Mikhail. Simple. Hedge blossomed. He could be quite a help. The very thought of the treadmill was too appalling. The grinding effort . . . he had short legs and would be forced to move very fast. It would undoubtedly kill him. But there was no need for all that. He had already thought for himself – or someone, Shard perhaps, had said it – that if the CAT faction happened to kill Mikhail before he went into action, a world wide sigh of relief would go up. And he himself would be an integral part of that relief. He would be fêted, rewarded – the Prime Minister would be so grateful. It might be as well, afterwards, if the existence of the treadmill could be concealed; it might give people ideas.

He said, "I think I can help."

"Great," Tex said. "So let's start."

*   *   *

There was that failure to appreciate the iron determination and sheer basic courage and right thinking of the British Prime Minister. This was manifested that evening in the Elysée Palace, but not until after a splendid state banquet attended by all the delegation leaders, Russian, German, Belgian, Italian, Danish, Irish, Netherlands in full evening dress with decorations. After dinner, Mrs Heffer had cleverly manoeuvred President Ligot into a tête-à-tête in order to discuss the forthcoming programme and the alterations initiated by the French.

The President had stated his position quite clearly.

"*Mais non, M'sieur le President,*" the Prime Minister said in an atrocious accent. She had another god besides Margaret Thatcher and this was Sir Winston Churchill, who had prided himself on his abominable French. To speak the language horribly had been one way of putting down de Gaulle in those wartime years of long ago. Having started her sentence in French as a courtesy, Mrs Heffer switched to English; President Ligot spoke the language well enough. "We must not appear to be cowards – "

"But Madame, the expediency – "

"I don't much care for expediency," the Prime Minister interrupted. She smoothed down the skirt of her dress. "And it's not just a dislike of namby-pambyism either. There's the question of Mr Hedge of my Foreign Office – as you know, he's been kidnapped on French soil, and – "

"Yes, yes, I am sorry."

Graciously Mrs Heffer inclined her head. "Thank you. Now, the deed's done. I'm told that Mr Hedge will undergo hardship, even death let's face it, if the original programme is not kept to. Well, we *can't* have that, can we?"

President Ligot closed his eyes and gave a barely-suppressed sigh. Damn the woman. He felt disinclined to mention expediency a second time. He said, "Much is at stake, Madame."

"Yes. Very likely world peace. Well, we can face up to that if we have to. I'm under no illusions. But whatever might, and I stress *might*, happen I simply cannot and *will not* sacrifice a *British subject*. And I don't suppose you'd really expect me to. Suppose it was a Frenchman. I ask you, what would your reaction be then?"

The President shifted restlessly and muttered something indistinct about *la France* and patriotism. The woman was as impossible as he'd known she would be – this was not their first meeting. And all this talk about facing up to the shattering of world peace, with its implication that Britain at any rate could take it . . . *mon dieu, how* long was it since the Falklands? That epic lingered still and its undoubtedly glorious mantle had descended upon Mrs Heffer as though inherited from Margaret Thatcher with the Premiership. At any moment the harridan might bring up the touchy subject of French supply of Exocet missiles to the Argentinians – she had a long memory. She also had him by the short hairs and he knew it. He knew it because his intelligence services had made a certain report to him: inside what the British thought of as the security of their Embassy Mrs Heffer had stridently announced to the Ambassador that if the French refused to consider the safety of a British subject, then she would at once withdraw the British delegation back to London. She would not be tactless enough to say this to the President after an excellent dinner, but it was known she *had* said it and it was in her face and President Ligot knew that Mrs Heffer never, never back-tracked. Once a thing was said, that was it. Besides, he'd always known that she meant to sabotage the conference any-way, if she could get away with it. She had never intended to allow the French notions of détente to prevail. Of course, she wouldn't get away with it once the conference started, but if she withdrew then the conference would never take place at all and *la France* needed the support of the other assembled delegates . . . no conference, no decisions. Back, as the British would put it, to square one.

Mrs Heffer was starting up again, her arguments neatly gathered in, like a harvest. Her voice shrilled, began to sound like a machine-gun; she fought her battles by a process of attrition. President Ligot's head spun; he was tired, strained – so much worry, so much to do, so much to think about always, even though he was not personally attending the actual confer-ence . . . and there was some opposition from within his own camp: his own Premier had been inclined to disagree about altering the schedule once set. His Premier was an angry man, fanatically anti-terrorist, and had had much to say about *crimes de sang* and the over-riding need never to be seen to give in, to be deflected by the men of blood. As the woman's voice went on, making his head ache, President Ligot knew he had to bring it to an end. He thumped the table. His hand shook. "*Yes, yes yes,* Madame! I agree. A British subject . . . the programme will stand as first announced. I shall give my orders."

What a fool the woman was, what a risk! It would be her fault entirely.

Mrs Heffer smiled. "*Thank* you," she said. The voice was warm now. "Including the trips on the river?"

"Yes."

First thing next morning, the orders went out from the Elysée Palace. Everything was put hastily into reverse and, by personal order of the President himself, the veil of secrecy was drawn tighter. Much tighter. Not so tight that the reversal failed to reach the outstretched ears of the man called Henri, who had alerted the cyclist from Paris. Henri hastened to pass the word on to Mikhail that the original plan could now be restored. But the word did not reach its destination. Henri, at a pedestrian crossing whilst en route for a safe telephone, was cut down by a taxi. His head was crushed by a bus, speeding up on the taxi's left-hand side.

*   *   *

The previous night, while Prime Minister and President were at dinner, the barge had reached the rendezvous where Mikhail was to meet the man he'd referred to as Stolnik. The barge went as it were to ground a few miles out of Paris, into the cover of a large boathouse in a disused boatyard. More precisely, a disused bargeyard . . . with the non-persons and their rifles, Shard was ordered out on arrival. The Kalashnikov was still in evidence, still held by Nicholas. By now Shard had been told his role: using the transceiver supplied by the Paris police, he was to pass false information, yet to be announced, at a time also yet to be announced. Failure to put on a satisfactory act, a convincing act, would result in his death. Simple enough. In the meantime the group sat on a concrete landing-stage inside the boathouse alongside the silent barge, presumably waiting for Stolnik. It was a very dark night; and there was no light in the boathouse. This was by Mikhail's order. Concealment, naturally, was all, and they were close now, or comparatively so, to Paris. Police could lurk. Mikhail was tense, his voice low but brittle as it came through the darkness. This, he seemed to be saying, was where the danger started. From now on, he said, there would be total silence.

There was; it was broken only by the sound of breathing. Once again little fat Annie was alongside Shard – by design, he rather suspected. The girl was a nympho and he possibly had some sort of attraction, however square he might be behind the hippie disguise which he still wore. A man was a man and the non-persons didn't look likely to have much sex appeal; they were too desiccated, skin and bone, walking skeletons who needed a decent meal, only just out of Russia and probably only by the skin of their teeth at that.

It was a long wait. From time to time Mikhail went outside and came back to report no sign of Stolnik. After a while Nicholas went out to keep extended watch. Mikhail was restless, very uneasy now. Shard's wrists were still tied; Mikhail wandered over to the door into the boatyard, wandered back, went away again, his footsteps muted as he moved on tiptoe.

In a low voice Shard spoke to little fat Annie. "Who's this Stolnik?" he asked.

She shook her head; she didn't know, or wasn't saying. Her hair fell across Shard's face, smelling of cow field. He asked, "What about Tex and his hippies? Still waiting for the UFOs, and heaven?"

She didn't know that either. Tex, it seemed, was old hat now. She didn't seem interested. There was certainly something mental . . . but she was interested in other things, things of more immediacy. Proximity, to little fat Annie, was all. Shard felt pressure on his thigh. Little fat Annie was like a cat, rubbing. It was dark and she couldn't help taking advantage. Mikhail's attention was concentrated wholly on the door, on the outpost provided by the old Russian, on the non-arrival of Stolnik.

Little fat Annie pressed harder, moving lasciviously. She wanted a response; but there was nothing Shard could do

140

about it, even if he wanted to, unless the girl was willing to assist. He said as much, in a whisper.

"Rope, Annie. On my wrists."

"Oh, yes, I know."

"Untie it, Annie."

The pressure stopped suddenly. She drew in a breath, then giggled. "Oh no. Mikhail would be angry."

"Yes, he would be."

"Promise you wouldn't tell?" she asked after a while.

When it came to the crunch, he couldn't do it to her. It was the way she had spoken, the odd trust in her voice. Poor, simple little fat Annie . . . Mikhail would flay her alive. He thought of Hedge, of the Russian delegation in danger. He had a duty, but in all probability he'd never get away with it in any case, never get past Mikhail or the Kalashnikov in the hands of old Nicholas. All he would do would be to ensure trouble for little fat Annie. The non-persons wouldn't have any scruples, any emotions probably. They had been dehumanised and the struggle to exist was all.

As it turned out, there was no need to involve the girl. He hadn't yet answered her question when Stolnik arrived, complete with transport. Engine sounds were heard distantly, coming closer. At the door, Mikhail was watchful behind his revolver. After a few minutes, by which time the on-coming vehicle had stopped, Nicholas came back. There was a brief conversation with Mikhail, then Nicholas went away again. The engine sounds were resumed, stopped again close to the boathouse. Nicholas came in with two more men. Orders were passed to the non-persons. Mikhail shut the door and flicked on a torch, played it over the men with the rifles, over a long, low barge. The non-persons got to work, opening up the cargo hatches and starting to unload. Case after case, the artefacts of terrorism. Shard stared. It was nothing short of an arsenal. Enough to blow a very big hole in Paris. And God alone could tell what Plan Two, the alternative, might be.

When all the stuff was out and piled on the concrete landing stage, Mikhail flicked off the torch, opened the door and went

141

outside. The darkness inside the boathouse was the more intense after the light from the torch.

This might be the only moment on offer. Shard took a big chance. Wrists still bound, he moved fast for the door, coming from behind the line of unloaded cases, using the faint loom of the outside air as his guide. Nicholas was by the door; Mikhail had moved right out to the lorry, with one of the new arrivals. Shard took the old man on the shoulder, something like a football-field charge. Nicholas spun round like a top and clutched for the doorpost. Shard ran like the wind, with no idea where he was going. There were sounds from behind, but subdued ones, and the phut-phut of silenced guns. The boatyard was littered with gear, discarded stuff, and it was still very dark, a mixed blessing. But Shard managed to keep on his feet, dodging around the piles of junk, round crummy buildings. Bullets smacked into rotting woodwork. One or two came close; he felt the wind, heard the angry buzz. But he was gaining on the pursuit: he was very fit and hard. The non-persons were not, and Nicholas was an old man. Ahead of him he saw the gateway, the exit from the boatyard.

Like a fast shadow, he went through. The gunfire followed him and bullets zinged and ricocheted but he made it. The pursuit wasn't showing itself beyond the gates: Shard was a valuable property all right, but Mikhail and Nicholas would be likely to find more trouble from any disturbance in the locality, such that would bring in the police. They wouldn't be taking risks and it had been obvious they were on the point of leaving the barge in any case. Shard found himself in a narrow thoroughfare, a street in what seemed to be a small town, or perhaps a suburb of Paris. The darkness was as thick as ever: there were no street lights. But he saw small shops, what looked like a boat chandler's store, a café, a food shop, a draper's. He heard running footsteps behind: someone as yet unseen was taking a chance after all. He dodged down a side street, ran into another that led across, then another and another, back and forth through the rabbit-warren; the footsteps could no longer be heard. Shard found a narrow alley and went in, breathing hard. The alley ran between two sordid houses, joined a cross-alley at the back. Shard moved past dustbins and heaps of filth, disturbed the mutual spitting of two tom-cats, then found a shed that turned out to be a latrine, a simple hole in the ground under a ramshackle roof. Here he waited until he considered it safe to emerge. Back again in a main thoroughfare after a while he found no-one about, not even a solitary nightworker making his way home, not a reveller rolling back from a party, not a policeman. At the end of the street he came upon a house with one wall fallen away, a derelict building looking like the long, long aftermath of war-time bombings. The bricks stood jagged, raw. He backed up to them, got his bound wrists into position and started sawing away at the rope. When the strands parted he went on, came to what seemed to be a main road.

He found a signpost: one way Rouen, the other Roissy. He was not far off Paris. Roissy, said the signpost, was two kilometres ahead. Call it a total of four miles and he would be in the capital. He walked on, swinging his arms, getting the circulation back. After around half an hour's walking he heard something heavy coming up behind. He dodged down into a ditch that ran alongside the road, which was now in open country. As the vehicle passed, moving at speed, he caught a glimpse of Nicholas in the cab. That was all: the number plate was unlit and he was unable to read it.

He came out from cover and went on.

★   ★   ★

"Frankly," Hedge said from the floor of the cellar, his mind still roaming fearfully around treadmills, "*everywhere*'s at risk. Or that's how we're looking at it. Even the Elysée Palace. Even the National Assembly – there's to be a reception there. And of course the routes through Paris. They'll be well watched, of course. But if you ask my opinion, I'd say this man Mikhail has a very wide field."

"Sure. You're here to narrow it down, right?"

"Yes," Hedge agreed.

"Go ahead, then. Narrow it."

"But I can't. It's Mikhail's choice, after all."

143

Tex stared at him. "Look. What's the official view of the most likely place? There's bound to be some place where the Frogs see, or think they see, a good chance for it to happen. That's what I want."

Hedge pondered frantically. The sweat was pouring still. His feet, his heart . . . he would never stand the strain even for five minutes, he knew he wouldn't.

"Come on," Tex said warningly.

Hedge said, "Do I take it you don't in fact know the whole programme for the visit?"

"Something like that. So cough. I guess we're getting a little warmer, aren't we."

Convicts used to be put in treadmills, the early nineteenth-century version of hard labour. Donkeys were put in them, to draw water and so on. Once, Hedge had seen one, in Carisbrooke Castle in the Isle of Wight – horrible! It would be an act of the most extreme cruelty and it wasn't fair . . . he gave a sound like a whinny and said, "Yes, all right, very well. I'll tell you – so far as I'm able."

"Great," Tex said, still staring like a gimlet, searching out lies. "Remember it's the changes I want to know about. Just in case the brass doesn't agree to sign your personal reprieve by restoring the original set-up. Got it?"

"You want to know what the new programme is?"

"That's what I just said, isn't it? If I were you, I wouldn't be playing for time. Time won't help you, Hedge. The tread-mill's patient, right?"

Hedge shook. Playing for time was all he could do; he had no idea in the world what the new proposals were, it had all been in the melting-pot when these people had kidnapped him, but Tex was never going to believe that a big shot hadn't been consulted in advance. Hedge said desperately, "Really, I don't see how it can help you whichever programme's decided upon!"

"Our worry, Hedge. I need to know so I have the best chance of getting a line on Mikhail Asipov."

"But he won't know either – won't know about any changes. So he'll stick – "

144

"I wouldn't bank on it. Talk, Hedge. Me, I'm not as patient as the treadmill." Tex lifted a hairy wrist and looked at his watch. "One minute, Hedge. Sixty seconds."

He began counting.

★   ★   ★

Shard called the Embassy by telephone from the first police station that he found on his route. Roberts-White, he was told by a minion, was not yet up – not surprisingly, since it was just after two a.m.

"Get him," Shard said. He waited. The First Secretary didn't take long, but sounded sleepy. Sleep vanished fast when he realised who the caller was. Shard passed the encapsulated facts and Roberts-White absorbed them fast.

"That barge. Better get it looked at," he said.

"The police are on their way. In the meantime, Mikhail's lot know the programme's changed – there was a leak, they have a plant, name of Henri, surname unknown – "

"Just – "

"Hang on till I've finished. I've found out some useful facts. There's a man called Stolnik, a Russian presumably. I suggest you check him out, see if he leads anywhere. In the meantime, I believe – I'm certain in fact – that the attempt was to be made while the Russian brass was on the river. Now that's out, seeing that the programme's apparently changed, and you can forget the river. It's the alternative plan now, whatever that is. I'm sorry I didn't get any info on that."

Roberts-White had been trying to get a word in all the way through. Now he said, "It's not so simple, old chap. The programme's on again. The *river*'s on again."

Shard was rocked. "What the bloody – "

"Our PM," Roberts-White said.

145

13

Hedge had been right: the American didn't believe him when he insisted he knew nothing about the changes. Big shots always had the facts, right?

"No," Hedge said, almost in a squeal. "I'm not – not such a big shot as you call it. I'm really not." He was close to panic, close to pleading abjectly for his life. There was just nothing more he could reveal and revelation would be the only way out of the treadmill.

And Tex was as good as his word. Hedge was propelled up the stone steps, through the heavy door at the top, made to turn to his right, walk along a dirty passage, and then down into another cellar, a larger one than the other and containing the dreadful instrument of torture, a huge wheel with steps in it, going round and round on an axle when Tex set it in motion by giving it a push.

"Electrically controlled," Tex said, "when connected up. Moves fast. Get in, right?"

"Please, no!"

"Going to talk?"

"I've told you – "

"Sure. So get in."

Hedge had to be forced in. He was heavy, but Tex was a strong man and was assisted by the lantern man, who was still around to cast light. Hedge was thrust in through a sort of bird's nest of wooden staves and spokes and Tex went across to a wall and fiddled with a switch in a metal box. The thing started up – fast, as Tex had said. Hedge's feet moved rapidly and he gave a high moan of utter despair.

*   *   *

When Shard reached the Embassy, Roberts-White was in his office and looking worried. There had been no word of Hedge; presumably, now that the kidnappers' terms had been met by Prime Ministerial intervention, he would be released. But so far there had been no communication from the Communist Alliance Transatlantic, and there was, naturally enough, no known avenue of making contact with them.

"No public announcement?" Shard asked. "About the scheduling reversion?"

"Good heavens, no."

"In Hedge's interest?"

Roberts-White shook his head. "Regretfully, no. Security has to come first – "

"But they all know the original programme," Shard pointed out.

"Yes, but there's nothing like a foxed enemy, don't you agree? Keep 'em guessing. I refer, of course, to Mikhail's lot – CAT will naturally be told when they make contact. In Hedge's interest, you see. Poor old Hedge," Roberts-White said without much conviction. "I doubt if they'll harm him, though." He added, "What do we do now? Any ideas?"

Shard let out a long breath. There was still all to learn; not a lot of progress seemed to have been made. He said, "Well, for a start, we can't disregard the river after all, evidently. Mikhail could get to hear about the Heffer antics – "

"Via Henri?"

"Yes. Did you get a line on who he might be?"

"Sorry. Not enough to go on. I met a brick wall."

"Stolnik?"

"Ditto. So far, that is. I have a man working on it."

Shard nodded. He said musingly, "There *is* another point, you know."

"Yes?"

"About the river. It could still be an impossibility from Mikhail's angle – seeing I got away."

"Yes, true. On the other hand, he might see it as his best bet notwithstanding, mightn't he? We wouldn't now be expecting him to go into river action." He ran his fingers through his hair. "The whole bloody thing's still wide open, really."

Shard agreed. The report from the police, when they had returned from the boatyard, was bleak: there was no barge. And no-one could be certain that the high explosive had after all left in the lorry. After Shard's escape, it could have been reloaded into the barge. Of all the men aboard that barge, Shard from his ditch had seen only old Nicholas in the lorry. His own belief from his observations had been that Mikhail's original intent had been to somehow or other impact the explosive-laden barge against the river boat carrying the Russian delegation on its sightseeing trip. This he put to Roberts-White, who regarded it as highly unlikely: the river would be under heavy and constant patrol and no other traffic would be permitted on the sections of river to be navigated by the VIPs. But the barge could, Shard said, be remote-controlled from the shore and could batter its way through any police interference, and then be blown, also by remote control, as soon as it had been manoeuvred alongside the pleasure boat. If the barge had indeed been reloaded it still could be. Mikhail had seemed in a foul mood on hearing about the changed programme; clearly enough, it had been a case of second best when he'd gone into his alternative. Now, Mrs Heffer could have played into his hands.

"She'd never live *that* down," Roberts-White said. He looked more worried than ever. Whilst in France, the Prime Minister's actions were to an extent an Embassy responsibility; after all, HE represented HM, a bigger fish than the PM . . . and HE was supposed to offer his advice, which often enough origin-ated from his underlings. It was all a great anxiety to a career diplomat and in any case Roberts-White had voted for Mrs Heffer and thought she was doing rather well. He would be sorry to see her vanish politically in a cloud of smoke basically engendered by the Soviet Union.

Shard said, "I'm going to take a look along the river."

"For what?"

"That barge. In the meantime I suggest you arrange for the police and troops to be on the lookout for anyone with what might be a remote control outfit – later, I mean, as the time gets nearer to that river trip. What time is it scheduled for now?"

"Which one – the day trip or the evening booze-up?"

"The first, primarily. The one with just the Russians."

"1500 hours tomorrow," Roberts-White said. "The other's also tomorrow – 1930 hours, both leaving from the quay below the Eiffel Tower. The Russians will be leaving in a motorcade from the Ecole Militaire – but you know that, of course."

Shard nodded. "Can you arrange a disguise? I'm kind of tired of being a hippie . . . and I could be spotted. Likewise for my WDC. I'll take her with me. I assume she's around?"

Roberts-White grinned. "Raring to see you again. I said I wanted a word first. What sort of disguise have you in mind?"

"Pure tourist. The respectable sort. A little facial alteration would help."

"Right." The First Secretary took up a telephone. "I'll fix it with the Police Judiciaire."

Inside ten minutes Shard was on his way with WDC Brett to the Rue de Saussaies. The job was done thoroughly and it took time. When they emerged Shard was smartly dressed – light-weight, cream-coloured coat, dark brown trousers, sunglasses, plus a revolting peaked cap in bright blue, far from his natural taste, and there were subtle differences in his face, nothing elaborate but very effective, at any rate at a distance. By this time he had put Eve fully in the picture as to Mikhail's set-up so far as he had observed it. She was intrigued by little fat Annie's inconstancy. Down in the hippie commune the girl had seemed totally absorbed by Tex, as later she had been absorbed by Mikhail.

Shard said, "She's anyone's Achilles' heel, is Annie." He was pretty sure he hadn't seen the last of her.

*   *   *

Hedge was near the end of his tether now. He ran on as the treadmill spun beneath his rapidly-moving feet. He had no breath even to repeat that he didn't know anything. This was

149

abominable torture, cruel and uncivilised. He was tormented. Sweat poured; his clothing was soaked. His heart thudded but so far had taken the strain. His face was like a beetroot.

The man Tex had watched for some while, grinning cynically, then he had called up the steps and another man had come down to take over. Tex had left. Tex had then crossed Paris to make a telephone call. The call was to the British Embassy. He spoke to Roberts-White. He said, "CAT."

"Yes?" The call would be monitored automatically, but Roberts-White didn't expect much. The conversation would be too brief.

"Agreement?"

"Yes. Full restoration."

"Right."

"What about our man?"

"He'll be okay – "

"We want his immediate release."

"You won't get it. I said, he'll be okay. But he stays till this thing's over – just in case." The call was cut. Roberts-White checked with the monitors. No luck. And already the caller would be legging it fast. He was. Tex went by Metro, back to Hedge's revolving cage. As he came down the steps, Hedge was in extremis. An obvious case of imminent collapse, and Tex didn't want him dead. Not just yet. He went across to the wall switch and flicked it and the treadmill stopped. Hedge lay inert on the treads, dripping sweat, speechless. Tex and the other man dragged him out. Gasping, he lay on the floor. No use questioning him; maybe, after all, he'd spoken the truth and didn't know anything.

*　　*　　*

The international brass was assembled for the first of the series of meetings. These were taking place in the Foreign Ministry and the place swarmed with security men and uniformed police. Outside the security was heavy. The public was being kept well clear, no chances being taken. Official Paris was in something of a ferment; the British Prime Minister had thrown an enormous stone into the pool and the ripples would

150

spread. President Ligot was in a bad mood when he opened the proceedings by making a lengthy speech of welcome to both east and west. He had been manoeuvred into a corner by Mrs Heffer and he was deeply regretting having caved in to her demands. The British were always a pestilential people, awkard, umbrageous over the smallest things, insular – almost more insular, if such were possible, ever since they had been admitted to the EEC. The words of President Ligot's speech were impeccably friendly but were given the lie by his tone and his manner of delivery. He was off his stroke. Russian faces stared back at him, blank and formidable as if they had come – like the British on this occasion – to say no to every-thing and never mind the French willingness to be helpful and block any British opposition. And Madame Heffer kept catch-ing his eye, making her feelings obvious, nodding sometimes her approval, at other times frowning and shaking her head and turning to whisper at her Foreign Secretary, who always agreed with everything she said.

She was very off-putting. President Ligot knew that this conference was going to turn sour, and he thanked God for the fact that his Prime Minister would be taking the brunt. As President of France he would not himself take part, but of course that didn't mean he would escape later consultation and the necessity of making final decisions and giving the seal of his approval to the wretched mouthings and falsely friendly utterances that would rise like steam into the air of the Foreign Ministry . . . and so much depended upon what was to be decided. France was moving towards the Soviet Union, doing her best to increase EEC trade with Moscow, to reduce the arms build-up, to stop all testing of nuclear devices of a warlike nature, to share more and more their combined power resources – gas, electricity – all in the interest of world peace and prosperity. But the British took an opposite view, all on their own in the face of the views of the rest of the EEC countries. Madame Heffer had said so, making no bones about it.

In order to stress her position once again at the last moment she had insisted on what she called a working breakfast.

Breakfast! She had invited herself coolly to the Elysée Palace that very first morning of the conference, stealing a march on all the others, especially the Russians of course. For President Ligot breakfast, which he normally enjoyed in bed, had been ruined. The woman had gone on and on, making point after point, ticking them off on her fingers. Détente was one thing and was all very well up to a point; all-out trade and power sharing was quite another and would do no more than encourage and enrich the Soviet Union who would go on preparing for war behind the scenes and then attack the west with what the west had given them. On and on and on. It had been terrible – terrible.

It, the very recollection of it, was impeding President Ligot's delivery. And it came to a dead stop when a person entered the chamber, clearly a person of some authority since he had been admitted by the security guards, and approached the British Prime Minister.

In the silence Mrs Heffer's voice could be heard quite clearly. "*What* did you say, Mr Roberts-White?"

There was another whispered consultation. "Rubbish!" Mrs Heffer said. "I *never* go back on my word. I think *everyone* knows that. Of course, I can't speak for others." Suddenly she seemed to become aware that President Ligot had stopped. She rose to her feet, giving a charming smile. "I'm so sorry, M'sieur le President, I do apologise. Please go on."

There was a stir among the delegates; Britain was not making herself popular, no bad thing for France perhaps. His face furious, President Ligot continued.

*　　*　　*

The Prefect of Police together with the head of the GIGN had called earlier upon the Ambassador. They had been polite but antagonistic behind the façade. The British were being a nuisance.

"It's out of my hands, gentlemen," the Ambassador said. "Yours too, I rather think. The order came from the President himself."

"Under pressure, yes."

The Ambassador shrugged. "It comes to the same thing, an order. Naturally, I back my Prime Minister – "

"Naturally, M'sieur. Also foolishly. The danger is so great. Your Superintendent Shard, he has spoken of a barge full of high explosive – "

"Yes. Not an unobtrusive weapon I would think. Easy to bowl out."

"Possibly. And of course, as such, may not be intended. Superintendent Shard may be quite wrong. There are so many other possibilities than a barge. And we have found no such barge, despite a most thorough search."

"Well, of course, they'll be keeping it where it won't easily be found," the Ambassador murmured, adding quickly, "But I take your point. What else have you in mind?"

"As I said, so many things. The Ecole Militaire, perhaps – "

"Well guarded."

"Yes, yes, M'sieur, but so is all Paris well guarded, all the relevant streets, the buildings . . . all except the river, which is guarded too, but is much more difficult to guard fully, do you not understand, M'sieur?"

The speaker, who was the GIGN man, was becoming almost hysterical, his voice rising with his busy shoulders. He went on, "I implore that you talk again with your Prime Minister. A change of heart – "

"No, that's out," the Ambassador answered briefly. "In any case, it's not her who's under threat, it's the Russians. Frankly, I suggest you approach them. If they withdraw from the river, surely that solves the problem?"

"But no. No, no, no! That is to say, M'sieur, yes, they have been approached. They say, firmly, no. If the British are willing to take a risk by attending the night trip, then so are they, both then and in the afternoon. What the British Prime Minister does, so also will the Russian Foreign Minister. It is an impasse. Please, please to intercede . . . as a matter of the greatest urgency, at once!"

The Ambassador had had no choice but to agree to that, though he knew very well what the answer would be. He had sent Roberts-White with his most urgent submission to the

Prime Minister. After that initial meeting was over, Mrs Heffer was driven to the Embassy. The Ambassador diffidently tried to justify Roberts-White's message, but was halted. Mrs Heffer was angry about Hedge.

She said, "My dear Stephen, don't talk nonsense. I deprecate very strongly any suggestion that we should change the programme again, and of course if we *did*, then it certainly wouldn't help Mr Hedge, you'll agree – "

"Yes, I – "

"Thank you, Stephen. Not that I don't think these people are *absolutely dastardly*. We must all do our best. But we simply can't use poor Mr Hedge as a bargaining counter any further than he's being used already by these wretched persons. I think that was your suggestion? Or one of your suggestions. That we should counter by *not* going along with them *unless* they released Mr Hedge as they'd promised?"

"Well – "

"Yes, it *was* your suggestion," Mrs Heffer said accusingly, "and I don't think it's worthy of you, Stephen."

*   *   *

At first Shard had no more luck than the police. There were a few river barges to be seen down towards Roilly; but the Paris section of the Seine had already been closed to all except essential traffic as a precautionary measure and almost the only movement was from police and military launches and the naval diving craft around the great supports of the bridges. None of the barges Shard found down river tallied with his knowledge of that used by Mikhail. Frankly, he was beginning to doubt his own hypothesis.

"Nothing would get through," he said. 'Not a hope!"

"What about the remote control idea?" Eve asked.

"Yes. I believed at first that would work and I suppose it still could."

"Then why the doubt, sir?"

Shard shrugged. "It doesn't quite tie up. Mikhail knows we're all on the alert now, obviously. Even if, as I thought might be the case, he still means to go ahead on the basis that we'll assume he won't – if you follow – I doubt if he could get a barge through far enough. It could be blown by gunfire long before it got anywhere near the closed area. And in fact I imagine that's what the French will have in mind to do."

They moved on, back for the car that the Paris police had provided. They looked like any tourists anywhere, strung with expensive cameras, binoculars, transistor radios, taking an interest in all they saw. Shard looked and felt baffled, the only thing to do being to wait and see – which meant they would probably be too late. As ever, so many possibilities apart from the river, but it was the river that still nagged away at Shard's mind. And Mikhail, naturally, had gone right to ground; the police hadn't picked up a thing, no leads at all. Likewise Tex, who would himself be trying to get a line on the Russian. It was the same as it had been from the beginning: find one and in time you were likely to find the other.

They drove back into Paris.

It was afternoon now: just about twenty-four hours to go before the Russian delegation embarked near the Eiffel Tower. "We'll just take a look around there," Shard said. By luck he found a parking space and they left the car. They went down some steps, drifted along the quay, past where one of the pleasure craft was embarking passengers. There was an ice-cream stall, a hot dog stall, and children playing, French children. They climbed back to the upper level, walked beneath the immensity of the Eiffel Tower; looking up, Shard had a curious sensation of falling backwards. On down towards the Ecole Militaire past August-dry gardens, feet scuffing over sandy paths. At the Ecole Militaire Shard studied the façade, walked down the sides, round the back. Big buildings, a very large area to cover – and already a lot of obvious security men around.

Mikhail was going to have his work cut out. But there was still the river. Really, the Prime Minister was being bloody obstinate. Eve seemed to sense his thought. She said, "I wonder if she's considered the Russians . . ."

"How?"

"That she's putting them at risk, sir."

"Only because they're just as obstinate. It's their choice as much as hers."

"Yes, I suppose so. One thing, she's got guts."

"Her strong point. And I admit that for all we know she may be playing this right. By which I mean we're very far from sure about the river, it's just a hunch. On the face of it, as we've seen, it's virtually impossible."

"So are the buildings. As long as no-one's been infiltrated."

They went back to the car. They drove to the Embassy. Shard went up for a word with the First Secretary and found Roberts-White on the security line. He was waved to a seat.

Ringing off Roberts-White said, "That was the police. You asked for a check on someone called Stolnik."

"Right."

"They've found a Stolnik. Russian, not unexpectedly. Member of a dissident group, exiled around twenty years ago. Lived in Paris ever since – quite well-known in toddlers' circles." Roberts-White grinned. "Ivan Stolnik, Russian toymaker."

"*Toy*maker?"

"It's over his shop front, apparently. Little place with workshop – he makes the things – in the Rue Gaspard." Roberts-White added, "I don't get the toy part, but the rest fits – doesn't it?"

"Yes," Shard said. "It does. Toys – he'd need to make a living, that's irrelevant."

"So what d'you suggest? Have him brought in and put under the grill?"

"I don't think so. Not yet. I'll just carry out a recce first. Where's the Rue Gaspard?"

"Montmartre. Not far from the Sacré Coeur."

"I'll go along and buy a toy," Shard said. "I've a feeling we could be getting warmer."

14

It was a grimy little shop in a grimy little street, and the fascia board with its message IVAN STOLNIK RUSSIAN TOYMAKER was faded almost into illegibility but perhaps it was a case of good wine needing no bush: there were three children with three adults in the congested premises. Shard went in with Eve; it was safe enough – Stolnik hadn't seen him back in the boathouse any more than he'd seen Stolnik. Behind a counter was a thickset man somewhere in his fifties, wearing a grey moustache beneath a big nose and hard, flinty eyes. He looked what he evidently was: an old-fashioned craftsman. Behind him was his workroom, a litter of wood and leather and stuffing and dye and paint and so on, all the ingredients for making rocking-horses, dolls' houses, arks, you name it, Stolnik made it and made it solidly, no modern trashy methods, no modern toys either.

One of the adults was an obvious grandmother complete with two poodles on leads. They were being a nuisance to everybody else but the grandmother was unperturbed; she was old France and haughty, scorning the *canaille*. Stolnik was being deferential. The old dame bought a rocking-horse for a rather uninterested small girl, paid for it as though throwing money to the poor, and Stolnik carried it out to an immense, hearse-like car waiting outside his shop on double yellow lines. There was a chauffeur, who got out to take delivery of the rocking-horse. Shard looked around: Stolnik was clearly a genuine toymaker whatever else he might be. Some of the toys were intriguing: boats for use in the bath, or on a pond . . . boats of all sorts, liners, sailing ships beautifully rigged – some of them were in bottles – warships with French colours, tiny rowing-boats, Chinese junks, even what seemed to be a US

Coastguard cutter of pre-war vintage. And so many other examples of Stolnik's skill: the dolls' houses were exquisitely furnished with beds, wash-stands, dressing-tables, chairs, bedside cabinets and so on.

Stolnik came back. He said something in French to the other customers and went through to the rear of his premises, opening a door into a back yard. Shard looked through; then he stiffened and put a hand on Eve Brett's arm.

"Let's go," he said.

"Not buying?"

"Not today," he said. They left the shop, not too fast, with backward glances at the stock.

"What was it?" Eve asked as they walked along the street.

He said, "Little fat Annie. In the back yard."

She drew a quick breath. "Did she see you?"

"No. I'm pretty sure not."

"So what now?"

"Full police surveillance," Shard said. "We won't go in – not yet. But from now on out, they won't move without being seen."

*   *   *

The French co-operation was as expected: one hundred per cent. It was efficient, too. Stolnik's premises were overlooked both back and front and surveillance could be carried out from the bedrooms of small hotels. Four plain clothes officers, two male and two female, booked into handy accommodation, as did Shard and his WDC. A strong squad of GIGN operatives was on close location and in radio touch with all the watchers and with HQ, and the latter was ready to send in reinforcements when necessary. Other agents were in the area, unobtrusively ready to put on tails when they got the word.

To Shard, it looked as though the net was closing. Or was about to. Just a question of time. Once Mikhail showed – if he did – then the moment would have come to go in. Meanwhile the first consideration was not to scare the birds away.

In position, the surveillance teams settled down for the watch. Shard and Eve were in a ground floor bedroom in one of the sleazy hotels facing the back of Stolnik's premises, watching from behind net curtains, aided by powerful binoculars. It could be a long business, boring until something happened. All that afternoon nothing did.

As the day began to drift into evening, at 1930 hours, little fat Annie left from the exit from the back yard. That was a surprise; little fat Annie wasn't the sort of girl any villain would let loose at such a late stage in the game. Shard, watching, saw one of the police tails latch onto her and saunter away behind. Three long hours later little fat Annie came back, this time with a different tail. The tail came into the hotel and was sent up. He reported that the girl had attended a disco, near the Champs Elysées. He couldn't be sure there hadn't been any contact. M'sieur, he said, would know discos. Noise and flickering colour, a press of bodies, all of them close. Shard knew, all right. And he made a fair guess that Mikhail was not on Stolnik's premises. If he'd been around, little fat Annie wouldn't have attended any discos, or anything else either, on her own. As he'd remarked earlier, the girl was a universal Achilles' heel . . .

Half an hour passed and then a small Fiat came slowly into the street below their window and stopped some distance clear. No-one got out. Just thirty seconds later the big doors of Stolnik's yard opened, there was a brief glimpse of little fat Annie doing the opening, then after a short delay a closed van emerged and turned away fast in the other direction from the Fiat. Having given the van a few seconds' start, the Fiat turned and followed, coming below Shard's window. Shard got a good view of the driver. He turned to Eve. "Did you see that?"

Eve nodded. "Tex, sir."

"Right!" Shard used his transceiver. Quickly after that a report came in that the van had been picked up and was being tailed from behind the Fiat. Shard's blood raced: things, at long last, were coming together and the sparks might fly now that Tex had, evidently, got his line on Mikhail. Or anyway Stolnik, which looked very much like the same thing.

*　　*　　*

Hedge had been removed from the treadmill's vicinity and put back in the original cellar with its overpowering smell of damp and decay. By now Hedge was almost abject, apprehending the grim loom of death, but there was no-one now to see. He had been left alone for some hours and he saw no hope. He had a feeling Tex and his associates had gone, shut up shop . . . and no-one in the Embassy had the remotest idea where this dreadful place was.

He would be left to rot.

He had climbed the steps and found the door locked. He had expected no less. Descending, he had slipped on the slimy stone and had gone all the way down on his bottom, which had upset him and shaken him up rather badly though there was no physical damage. He sat now with his back against the wall, in total darkness since the lantern had not been brought back. He sat and moaned, a sort of keening to demonstrate his fright, pathetically, to the empty air.

There was not a sound from above, from anywhere around. He had been so right: he'd been abandoned. They hadn't even bothered to question him again. They were going back on their promises and he just didn't matter any more. He'd been bypassed.

Then he heard a sound, very faint. It wasn't coming from above and it wasn't footsteps. It wasn't anything human, he believed. Nor animal either.

He listened intently, all his senses on the alert in an attempt to identify the sound. Tinkle, tinkle . . . trickle?

Hedge gave a gasp.

Water?

Yes, water he was certain.

Goodness gracious – water! Another infernal torture. But he was, he knew, not far from the Seine. Perhaps that was it; relief flooded as he told himself that of course it must simply be the tide – but *was* the Seine tidal? Not so far up as this – no. At least he didn't think it would be. The movement of boats, then? Or possibly a fountain somewhere. Or drains . . . what a thought! The French were filthy. It could even be one of those dreadful, impossible holes in the ground concealed by corrugated iron walls that in some parts of France passed for lavatories and you had to aim straight or squat over them and hope for the best. So insanitary, if it was Britain Borough Housing and Health would go mad . . .

But it wasn't that either.

The sounds increased to a gurgle, louder and nearer, and within minutes of that Hedge felt the wetness, the encroaching water. It lapped his bottom and he got to his feet with a shriek. Of course, there was no-one to hear him. He shook with fear. If the water deepened he would drown like a rat. It was no doubt intentional, all arranged that he should. Within the next five minutes he knew the water was deepening. It was now lapping over his shoes.

He began praying.

It was cold as well as wet. After a while Hedge found himself shivering uncontrollably. The rise in the water-level was slow but apparently inexorable. *Was* it the tide?

If so, it would go away again, though it might be so deep as to finish him off before it did. And he still didn't believe in the tide. No seaman, no riverman, Hedge knew little of tides except that they came and went with a curious predictability, but he felt he couldn't rely on easy salvation from a doubtful French tidal system. He had to do something, but what?

He could climb the steps. He'd be safer higher up; he did so, and sat trembling violently at the top, wondering why he hadn't thought of it earlier. He thundered on the heavy, impenetrable door. No response, just nothing but the awful silence broken only by the water's gurgle. It was gurgling *in* something . . . water didn't *gurgle* unless made to. Placid water, even rising placid water, didn't normally gurgle. Perhaps it was coming through something narrow, gurgling as it emerged into the wider cellar – something like that.

Panic! He must stiffen himself, he must not give in. Life beckoned. He forced his mind to happier things – the Embassy, the Foreign Office in distant, safe London. Whitehall and Downing Street . . . oh, if only the Prime Minister hadn't decided to come – but no, it wasn't her they were after . . . or *was* that American, Tex, after her as he'd

161

reflected some time in the past? The man was a communist. One never knew with communists. At least Mrs Heffer was keeping his thoughts off death and his predicament, but of course just as soon as that thought came into his mind so did the other, the death and predicament back again.

Possibly he should make an examination of the walls. Quite obviously, the water must be seeping through the walls. Unless it was rising from the floor, a sort of hole-in-the-ground lavatory in reverse. It could be that.

Hedge eased himself down the steps and splashed into the water. As his movement disturbed it the stench arose, stiflingly, horrid, full no doubt of disease. Hedge retched and went on retching, feeling desperately ill. But bravely he trod through the water, seeking some sort of hole. He found none. He tried again, to make sure. No hole.

It must be the walls.

Trying not to breathe more than he had to, he moved around the walls, feeling, probing. He had an idea that perhaps the water wasn't really meant to come in; there might be some shaky brickwork that was admitting it, brickwork that had deteriorated over the years. The building was, as he'd noted earlier, very old. It could be very crumbly. And the cellar had been more than ordinarily damp; it might have been seeping through on a minor scale for a long time. But if so, why had it run away again? Logically, the cellar would have filled up. Well, there must be a drain hole – but he hadn't found a hole. That was a mystery; he came away from the wall he was feeling and tried again for a hole in the ground; a hole would provide reassurance that he might not drown after all.

And yes, there was a hole: he hadn't found it before because it wasn't in the floor, it was in the side of the otherwise solid stone steps. A hole with a grating over it.

That could, and in fact did when he listened carefully, explain the gurgle. The water was gurgling away but not quite fast enough. The level was increasing. It was up to his knees now. The ingress had to be found. A nasty thought: perhaps he *had* found it.

162

In panic Hedge resumed feeling. He wondered what the time was. It must, surely, be night outside.

*   *   *

"They've simply not contacted," Roberts-White said to the Counsellor. "Not a peep."

"I wonder how Hedge is making out."

"Oh, he'll be all right. They've an obvious use for him still, haven't they? I'm not worried." Roberts-White went over to a polished mahogany corner cupboard and brought out a bottle. "Whisky?"

The Counsellor nodded. "Thank you, yes. Plain water."

Roberts-White poured. "Good health," the Counsellor said. "And a quick conclusion to all this bloody hassle. What about Shard?"

"Nothing fresh, not since the Fiat and the van."

"Not much time to go now." The Counsellor paused, sipped at his whisky. Very welcome; he'd had a long and tiring day. Mrs Heffer's presence in Paris had been like a gale sweeping through the Embassy and disturbing everyone's routine. Hedge was lucky to be out of it, nothing to do but wait for his release, though if anyone did happen to blow up the Russian brass he just might never be seen again. An act of revenge . . . the Counsellor shrugged. Such things were endemic to Hedge's job and he would be prepared for it. He went on, "I hear the Soviet Foreign Minister's rampaging."

"Oh? What about?"

"Security."

"On the river?"

"Yes. He wants so much protection the press of agents'll be in danger of sinking the bloody boat."

"Cold feet?" Roberts-White asked lifting an eyebrow sardonically.

"Could be."

"Don't say there's going to be *another* change of schedule. We have to think of Hedge, you know!"

The Counsellor grinned. "*We* do. The Russians don't."

Roberts-White was about to say something further when

163

his security telephone burred. He took it, looked up at the Counsellor who had been on the point of leaving for bed: it was getting late. He said, "Report coming through from police HQ . . . looks like a balls-up."

It had been a balls-up all right and a bloody one and across Paris in Montmartre Shard's reaction was fury when an agent came in with the news. But it had been the French who had suffered the casualties and he had to hold back on criticism. The van had stopped suddenly and Tex in the Fiat had reacted quickly and pulled past, very neat. From ahead a big Volvo had appeared, and had done a rapid U-turn. As the unmarked police car had crash stopped, the van doors had been flung open and a sub-machine-gun, query Kalashnikov, had sprayed bullets back. All but one of the plain clothes men had died, virtually cut to ribbons by the rapid rate of fire and the police car's tyres had gone as had its radio communication after an initial alarm call had gone out. When the alarm was answered and more cars went in they found the wreckage and nothing else: there was nothing in the back of the van. Nothing and no-one.

"And the Volvo?" Shard asked.

"Gone, M'sieur."

"And the men – and the girl, probably – with it. Number?"

But the number was not known. The man who had survived hadn't managed to get it. And the Fiat had vanished. The Fiat's number had, of course, been noted and it would be found. Fine, Shard thought cynically, but when it is, Tex won't be in it any more. "Now we go in," he said. "Stolnik's emporium might give us a lead – and might not!"

Not unexpectedly, they found the premises empty. Of people, not of stock, which was there in plenty. Shard wasn't especially interested in the toys. Eve Brett was; she had small nephews and nieces. This wasn't the time to look for birthday presents, Shard said, noting the interest. But he didn't repeat that when something caught the WDC's eye in a workshop, not the one in the front behind the counter but in a biggish shed opening off the yard at the back.

"Look, sir," she said. She pointed. There was a lot of

unfinished work around, the same sort of things as Shard had seen on his first visit. What had attracted Eve Brett's interest was a pile of lead sheeting; and lead in another form as well. A case with five lead canisters shaped like the small CO_2 bottles used to fill soda syphons or sodastream machines but much larger – about a foot in length, around eighteen inches in circumference, stubby. She moved towards them; Shard stopped her.

"Leave it," he said sharply. He got down on hands and knees and studied one of the bottle-shaped objects at close quarters. In its nose was a round hole a little under an inch across. There was a cylindrical cavity, perhaps three inches in depth and of the same circumference as the aperture. The other four had closed ends.

Shard got to his feet, frowning.

"What is it, sir?" Eve asked.

"I don't know for sure. I'm not taking chances. We'll get the army in. Maybe I'm being fanciful . . . but I've a hunch those things take a nuclear filling."

Eve stared at him in consternation. He said, "I hope I'm wrong, but . . . remember I told you Mikhail had all the high explosive offloaded from the barge in that boathouse? He wasn't going to need that once he'd been forced to shift to his alternative plan."

"You mean these are the alternative?" she asked.

He nodded. "Could be. It's just guesswork. We simply don't know. Another thing we don't know is whether or not Mikhail knows the original schedule's been restored. Or even if he could have decided to use these gadgets for *either* of his alternatives . . ."

"He could have some of these aboard the barge?"

He said, "Could be. This is a pack of six bottles, obviously. So one's missing. And another has its filling missing." He turned away. "We'll get the army in pronto."

15

They waited until the army arrived. A truck drove up, no time lost once Shard's warning had gone in, and the crate of canisters was taken away, incarcerated in a lead container as a precaution. A police presence was left to carry on surveillance in case anyone came back to the premises. Shard and Eve went back to the Embassy and Roberts-White was dug out of bed.

Shard's report rocked him. A nuclear explosion in the heart of Paris couldn't be contemplated; but it seemed it might have to be. He said, "I'll have to inform HE at once."

"Wait for the army to report back," Shard said. "Any word of Hedge?"

"No."

"Anything else? Tex? No leads?"

"Not a thing. Ditto Mikhail." Roberts-White paused. "Just one thing that may or may not connect. I have that hippie commune in mind."

"Well?"

The First Secretary said, "We have reports of hippies coming into Paris. Bloody great dollops of them – "

"Where from?"

"All points of the compass. Noisy. Soul, pop, folk groups, you know the sort of thing. Otherwise peaceful enough . . . it's the sheer numbers that are worrying the police, bearing in mind the current Paris scene."

"Are they congregating?"

"Not up to the last report," Roberts-White said. "They're still spread, camping in the open spaces, even in the streets. The police are keeping the Champs Elysées and all motorcade routes clear as best they can. It's an uphill task, I gather. Do you see any significance in the hippies?"

Shard said, "There could be a Tex connotation."

"That's what I wondered." Just then a telephone burred and Roberts-White answered. He looked up at Shard. "For you," he said. "Police HQ."

Shard took over. "Shard here." He listened, nodding at intervals. When he rang off his face showed relief. He said, "It's not nuclear. Just a new type of detonator. But God knows what they're supposed to detonate."

"And Stolnik has two of them with him – one of them being still in its container?"

"Right," Shard said.

*   *   *

Following Shard's report another attempt was made by the Ambassador to deflect the Prime Minister from the river excursion. The Ambassador telephoned early but the Prime Minister was awake, was up, and was on the ball. She said, "But Stephen, it's all still supposition."

"Shard's report – "

"Yes, Stephen. I understood *perfectly* what you said he said. It still remains unsubstantiated that these people mean to use these detonators *on the river*. They could use them *anywhere*, couldn't they?"

"Yes, that's true, but – "

"Then we're *all* at risk wherever we may be. Aren't we, Stephen?"

"Yes!" the Ambassador said, coming close to a snap. "But – "

"Well, then." The Prime Minister was calm, reasoned, unflappable, patient. "You know – the thing to do is to find these people before they can act. Then the problem's solved. In the meantime we must all carry on as usual and not be panicked. I say again, these devices can be used anywhere. The only really safe – and cowardly – thing to do would be to abort the conference and let all the delegations go home. I can't even *consider* that, Stephen."

"But – "

"And there's still Mr Hedge, remember." Steel had come

167

into Mrs Heffer's voice now. She was very British; and the British did not retreat. The Ambassador saw that it was hopeless and gave up the struggle for commonsense. In a way he had to admit she was right. It could happen anywhere, not just in jollification. Shard seemed set on the river, but in point of fact he had nothing more than that barge to go on, the barge that even Shard had admitted had been rejected by Mikhail in favour of an alternative plan. The mere fact that the river trips, one Russian and one with all the delegations, were taking place after all might throw all the terrorists' plans out of gear. Possibly, the Ambassador thought, that was what the Prime Minister had in mind . . .

★   ★   ★

Results, of a sort, had attended Hedge's feeling around the cellar walls: he found a crumbly patch where the bricks and their cement pointing were loose.

That was where the water was coming in.

Where something came in, something could get out. That was axiomatic. Of course water was water and always found a way into everything, or almost everything. But the brickwork was certainly crumbly and might succumb.

Hedge, hope rising, tore at the wall. He knew not what he might emerge into, but anything was better than being abandoned in the cellar, which would, he was convinced, mean certain death. Spurred by his fears he worked hard. The wall wasn't as crumbly as he had first believed; it resisted quite strongly. But after some time he managed to free a brick, and then quite quickly another came away and he was able to thrust an arm through.

There seemed to be an empty space behind.

Now the water was coming in a gush, fast enough perhaps to overcome the drain hole's capacity to take it away before it reached the roof. The gurgling was horrible, so was the smell. Sewage, river water, Hedge couldn't tell. He worked away in the darkness like a demon, hands torn and bleeding. This he scarcely noticed; life, fresh air, freedom was his all. He had no idea how long he had been in frenzied action when a whole

168

section of bricks fell away and when he felt around he found there was a hole large enough for him to go through. Water poured like a cataract over the lip of this hole as he clambered across, felt with his feet, and found solid ground at the bottom. The relief of getting out of the cellar over-rode his fear; but not for long. God alone knew where he was, what he was in. If only he had a torch. But the only way was forward and he reached out a tentative foot. It seemed clear ahead. He dragged his trembling body on against the flow of water. A few moments later he heard an alarming sound behind him, a sound of collapsing walls he believed it was. It went on for a long time and while it was happening something hard and solid took him in the small of the back, and he gave a yelp. He went ahead as fast as possible; the sound stopped. Now his rear was most likely cut off and if the way ahead was also blocked he would be as imprisoned as before.

★   ★   ★

Reports reaching the Embassy via the Paris police indicated that the hippies were now massing. The movement had started with the dawn and by now, mid-morning, was proving a severe embarrassment to security, who were tending to be overwhelmed with dirty bodies and music. The theme was peace, but Shard doubted if it was simply a demo against American missiles, NATO and so on. There had to be a Tex connexion, perhaps an attempt to occupy the police, to divert attention. The hippies couldn't be disregarded. The massing was taking place around the Eiffel Tower, between there and the Ecole Militaire, and along both banks of the river. The police had managed to keep the bridges clear, but the hippies had taken over the rest. Hopefully they could be cleared before the Russians embarked in their pleasure boat. Urgent contact was made with the Soviet Embassy; Ambassador spoke to Ambassador. The British suggestion, made unofficially behind Mrs Heffer's back, was that the Soviet should cancel. *Niet*, the Soviet Ambassador said. The hippies were peaceful and were by no means enemies of the

Soviet Union. There was nothing to fear from that direction. The British Ambassador made the point that that might be so but there was still everything to fear from the assassination angle. But he failed to shake his Soviet counterpart. He saw that the thing had gone far beyond a simple pleasure trip. It was a challenge, a gauntlet thrown down, a matter of national pride. Of intransigence, really. East against West, with France in the middle. Nobody was going to be the first to back down.

* * *

Shard and Eve circulated amongst the hippies. Once again, they were dressed for the part, just two in the mob, which certainly seemed peaceful enough. There was a carnival atmosphere and the pop groups were in full cry, ignoring the police who were hopelessly outnumbered. Paris, Shard thought, had probably never seen anything quite like it. Fornication, like in the commune down south, was taking place openly and a large number of other couples were stark naked, parading about, swaying, dancing, singing. There were banners about peace and love, banners against war and the arms race, banners for or against almost everything. Against blood sports, Mrs Heffer, unemployment, race prejudice; for free love and the GLC – these were the British, and there were many more in French, German, Spanish, Italian and even what looked like Arabic.

Here and there in the side streets police vehicles stood ready with grim-faced uniformed crews. Fire appliances were dotted about. Water-cannon were in evidence, but it would take all the water out of the Seine to damp down this mob, as Shard remarked to Eve as they pushed their way through along the Left Bank.

"If they go into action," he said, "they'll be torn apart."

Eve gave a breathless nod; however peaceful at the moment, the hippies held brooding menace, a potentially unstoppable force. It was claustrophobic. The air was heavy with the acridity of human sweat. The sun blazed down to make it worse. They pushed on from the Pont d'Arcole towards the

Pont d'Austerlitz, coming into the commercial port of Paris, the part where the barges could be expected, barges – the legitimate ones – loaded with Flanders coal and steel, building stone, timber from the Vosges, all manner of cargoes brought to Paris by a great network of rivers and canals. But since the day before all movement on the river had been halted; between them Mrs Heffer and the Russian Foreign Minister were being a hindrance to trade.

They moved, slowly, along the Quai de la Tournelle. They were approaching the Pont de Sully leading from Ile St Louis when Shard caught sight of something familiar. Something that *could* be familiar: a very thin hippie, male, with a pronounced limp. The one, he believed, who had shared food with them at the commune near Bourg St Andéol.

★   ★   ★

There had been another telephone call to the British Embassy: the Prime Minister for the Ambassador, personal, urgent. Mrs Heffer had reached another decision, an alarming one.

"Oh, Stephen. I'm going to join this afternoon's river trip. With the Russian Foreign Minister . . . yes. No, I'm adamant. *Of course* I realise the difficulties I'm making, and *of course* I appreciate there's some risk but I really do think not much. Not if I'm there, you see. Oh yes, yes, I know all that, Stephen, but don't forget it's the *Russians* who are under threat, *not me*. I feel it's up to me. No, Stephen, I'm *not* asking for your approval, I'm simply *informing* you." There was some more rather splenetic talk about it being up to her to wet her own toes as well as the Russians since it was she who had insisted on the restoration of the agreed schedule and then she rang off. It was only after she had done so that it came to the Ambassador that what the Prime Minister was about to do was in a sense a change from the original programme and that it might rebound onto Hedge. At once he called her back but was told she was unavailable. He tried twice more at intervals with similar results and was then forced to accept the inevitable. With no expectation that it would get him anywhere, he left a message with the PPS.

He sat back, his face deeply troubled. He had to admire courage but refused to admire obstinacy.

★   ★   ★

Shard and Eve Brett had approached the lame hippie, coming up through the mass of people. The hippie had sat himself down with his back against a wall. Shard squatted beside him on the dusty, sandy ground.

"We meet again," he said.

"Again?" The face was blank.

"You shared your breakfast with us. Not many days ago."

"Yes, man, I remember now."

"You were a friend in need. Maybe you can be that again." Shard was well aware of the risk he was taking; the hippie would remember something else: the fracas with Tex, the fact that it had been to do with Shard, and then the arrival of the police from Bourg St Andéol and the break-up of the commune. But time was running down: three hours, a little over. It was a time for desperate measures and the lame hippie was his only link with Tex. The same principle held: find Tex and you had the best chance you'd ever get of finding Mikhail, finding him in time. He said, "All these people. What's the idea?"

The hippie said, "The word spread, man. The word spread."

"From Tex?"

"Yes, from Tex."

"That he wanted you all here in Paris?"

"Yes, man, that's right, in Paris."

"And he's in Paris?"

"Yes, man."

"Where, right now? Do you know?"

"No, man, I don't know."

"Do you know what you're all here for?"

"To witness a big event, man."

"What event?"

"I don't know, man. No-one knows. We answered the call."

172

Shard glanced up at Eve, then back at the hippie. He asked, "How did the call come? By magic – or UFO?"

"Not magic, man, or UFO." The hippie was speaking as if he were in a dream, or maybe some sort of drug-inspired haze. They all seemed to be the same, had largely been the same back in the commune. The hippie went on, "By messenger, man. We were to be here, that's all."

Shard blew out his breath. He was getting nowhere. He did some rapid thinking. Guesses were all he had. Tex would possibly, probably, have made plans long ago against a police raid happening sometime in the commune . . . he would in that case have made his dispositions ahead, indicating some other gathering places where the hippies – legions more of them now than had been in the commune during Shard's visit – could be reached with messages after he'd scarpered, though no reports, to Shard's knowledge, had been made of such gatherings. No doubt there were remote spots in the south of France, deep valleys and such where few other people went and hippies could lie up. But to order his battalions to come here, to the river bank itself . . . that had to indicate one thing positive: Tex had known all along what Mikhail's plans were, time, place, the lot.

Not impossible. He would have his contacts. He wouldn't have gone into this thing unprepared, that was for sure.

Shard believed he wasn't far now from the heart of it all. But what, really, was Tex's reason for the gathering? To impress his followers with the 'big event', just that? A kind of heralding, an earnest, of the day the UFOs would come?

Crazy!

No, it had to be the diversionary aspect. The big crowd, the police helpless, everyone getting in the way of everyone else, and Tex could carry out his murder mission against Mikhail and the Avengers of St Petersburg and then get clear away in the mob.

Jerk the hippie to his feet, march him off for questioning? He'd never get clear of the crowds, like the police if they tried to make arrests he'd be torn to pieces. In any case, he didn't believe the hippie knew any more than he'd already said. He

173

was no big shot, not close to Tex like Frigger and Tom Tit still uselessly in police custody. He was cannon fodder.

Irresolution set in. So near and yet so far. Under three hours now, so many lives in the balance, to say nothing of what would be the spreading tidal wave of trouble in diplomatic relations afterwards.

Suddenly the hippie got to his feet, lurching on the lame leg. Emotion shone from his face, a kind of reverence. He was staring over Shard's shoulder. Shard felt the hair rise on the back of his neck.

He turned.

In the centre of a group of hippies, Tex. Tex in hippie gear but no stetson. Tex who could merge inextricably with his followers but was immediately recognisable to Shard.

Their eyes met.

Tex grinned. He came forward, hands on hips, lounging across the dust. He stared into Shard's face, into Eve's. He said, "I reckoned we might meet again. Come. With me. No tricks. You wouldn't get away with it. I guess you know that for yourself, though. Right?"

16

"Something," the Ambassador said, "must be done, M'sieur."

A spread of hands. "But what, M'sieur?" The Prefect of Police felt battered from many sides at once. The Embassy, the Elysée Palace, the Ministry of State for the Interior, the British Prime Minister and the Russian Foreign Minister, not to mention the GIGN. Some were for one thing, others for another. It was a madhouse, was Paris . . .

The Ambassador said, "Clear the hippies away. Oh, I know it's easier said than done, but – "

"It is impossible, we have not the men, M'sieur. We have not! I have said many times. And the hippies – they are peaceful – "

"Yes, at the moment – "

"They will remain so, M'sieur! I am positive, I am convinced. Banners of love and peace . . . no, M'sieur, I beg of you, do not teach me my job. I know all about façades, false faces, the evil of mankind is not a closed book to me, the Prefect of Paris Police."

"No, of course – "

"I believe it is only a demonstration. A demonstration against war, made for the benefit of the Russian Foreign Minister, M'sieur. That is all. And now, though this they will not know, the British Prime Minister as well, a fine opportunity – I do not condone it, naturally, but the presence of the hippies is a fact and must now be accepted."

The Ambassador sighed, got up from behind his desk and walked over to the window. It was a very hot day; Paris lay brown and dusty. The roar of traffic came up; the streets were thronged, but there were no hippies to be seen in the vicinity

175

of the Embassy. The river was the magnet: and what in God's name was going to happen that afternoon? The French seemed almost to be unserious, at least that was the impression given by the Prefect of Police. Leaving the window, the Ambassador spoke of the diversionary aspect referred to by Shard: no avail. That was unimportant, was met with shrugged shoulders. Why make a diversion at the very scene of the crime – if it was to be the river, surely the diversion would be elsewhere? There was no satisfactory answer to that. When the Ambassador made the point that a press of hippies would impede the security men, the Prefect, with yet another shrug, simply returned to his point about the absolute impossibility of clearing the banks by force. They did not want police-inspired bloodshed with the Russians in Paris. The real trouble, he said snappishly, was the foolishness of the politicians, east and west.

There was no satisfactory answer to that either.

★   ★   ★

Force majeure, the simple proximity of so many bodies: Shard had gone along with Tex, no option. Tex had removed his police-issued automatic and his pocket transceiver. With his protective group around him still, Tex sat down on the quayside, right above the river, the deserted river apart from a handful of small boys and girls sunning themselves and playing with model boats controlled by long sticks from the quay on the other bank, not a commercial quay but one that seemed to be a sunbathing spot beneath a high wall. The hippies hadn't penetrated there, and Shard guessed the area would be cleared of children before much longer.

Tex asked, "Going to watch the fun?"

"What fun?"

Tex laughed. "Guess you know that."

"Mikhail?"

"Right. Doing everybody a favour, that's me."

"By killing Mikhail?"

"Yeah. Any objections?"

"Not really," Shard said. "Except that I'm a policeman. Are you sure you can get him before he goes into action?"

176

"Yeah. Dead sure."

"How?"

"You'll see. I'm not saying anything yet. Just in case." Tex picked up a stone, flung it into the river. There was a plop, and ripples spread. Symbolic? Shard could hardly believe that it was going to happen, any of it. The day was too bright for death and destruction. He asked if Tex knew what Mikhail's plan was. Tex said he knew all right. Little fat Annie had got the word through. When? The precise detail, the final work-out – had that been a recent revelation? Yes, Tex said, it had. Very.

Like a disco?

Tex gave a brief laugh. "Sure, like a disco."

"Was little fat Annie a plant?"

"Well, not exactly a plant. More a go-between, I'd call her. Not too bright . . . but she sure has a big place in her heart for me, right?" Tex laughed again. "Annie, she'd rat on anyone to keep in cahoots."

"With you?"

"Sure, with me. All that was needed was a phone call."

Shard watched the sunlit river scene, wondered what, if Mikhail's plan should go ahead despite Tex, it would all erupt into. He asked, curiously, why Tex was so intent on killing Mikhail. Just to save the Russians? There could have been other ways of doing that; all Tex had had to do was pass the positive word to the Russian Embassy and that, presumably, would have been that – so long as they believed him.

Tex said, "Sure. And yes, it's personal. Two birds with one stone."

"You're running it a shade close."

Tex yawned. "Come again?"

"I mean, you could have killed him any time before now, before the end. And made sure."

"If you say so. I like this way."

Shard thought, it's all of a piece: the God-aspect in the commune, the elaborate hoax of the UFOs, the exhibitionism that was part and parcel of Tex, the drama of saved Russians coinciding with the death of an enemy. Why an enemy? What was that personal angle?

Tex said, "Remember Asipov? Stanislav Asipov, back in London?"

"I do."

"Mikhail's dad. An undercover dissident, never known as such to the Soviet authorities, right? Not till he tried to do a bunk out." Tex threw another stone into the Seine, watched until the ripples had died.

"So what?"

"He'd been in the States, right? Maybe you didn't know that. Doing some dirty work . . . very dirty. To make it brief, he killed my old man. Never got it pinned on him, of course. Not as murder, which is what it was. He got my old man in the shit with the FBI – informed on him, right? Denounced him . . . this was a long while after McCarthy, but they still don't like Reds back in the States." One more stone went in. "The FBI moved in and there was a gun fight. My dad got it . . . took a long while to die, and they didn't give him any help, no drugs . . . they just wanted him to talk. He didn't. He just died. But Asipov got protection because he'd informed. No-one ever knew who'd done the informing."

"Except you."

Tex nodded. "Right. Except me. And the FBI. I got to hear – from an FBI agent. I'm good with a gun."

"I get the picture. Why did Asipov inform on your father?"

Tex said, "Because Asipov wasn't a com. Just the same, he wanted to go back to Russia at that time and he wanted to go back with a nice, clean record to show the Kremlin. Still a good com, see? So his name was kept out of it. But he was still a dissident, an anti-com."

Shard asked, "Why do you want to take it out on the son? It was hardly his fault."

Tex grinned. "Mikhail's a dissident too, right? And that's the way I'm made. A guy has to have his revenge somewhere, right?"

Shard didn't answer; the question had been rhetorical.

178

Agree or disagree, it wouldn't make any difference to Tex. Shard asked, belatedly, about Hedge.

"Hedge is okay," Tex said. He pointed across the river. "He's over there, not far back from the quay. He's safe."

"When is he going to be released?"

Another grin. "Want him back? I'd say he's not much use to anyone . . . I thought he was a real big shot, but now I doubt it. Whiners don't become big shots, right? He's okay. He'll be turned loose when it's all over."

But on the other side of the river Hedge, in his own view, was very far from being okay. The tunnel, which it had turned out to be – so far as he could feel in the intense darkness – was long, narrow, and very frightening. For all he knew it might lead nowhere, but it was all he had. He shook like a leaf as he laboured on his way, pulling his body over obstructions, bumping his head cruelly, scraping his shins – his clothing was in tatters now – and still hearing water. Some way back, not far in from the cellar, his route had climbed a little and the run of water seemed now to be below him somewhere, which was fortunate. The fear of drowning had lessened, but the fear of entombment was even greater. An appalling death if it came that way. People who went potholing were mad, like mountaineers. Years ago the youthful Hedge had been taken by his father down the White Scar cave system in Yorkshire. The nightmare was with him still and was making his imagination a thing of utter horror. There had even been an underground waterfall. He might fall willy nilly down some long shaft and end up in the Paris sewers . . .

He struggled on, whimpering with fear.

*　　　*　　　*

The night before, using the Volvo after it had taken Stolnik and little fat Annie off the van from the toyshop yard, Mikhail had arrived at his ultimate destination. Old Nicholas had got there before him, with the blank-faced non-persons: the destination was in the commercial port. Under cover of a warehouse a packing-case was removed from the boot of the Volvo and stowed behind some piled empty crates.

179

"The barge?" Mikhail asked.

Nicholas said, "Down the river. Hidden until the morning." Mikhail nodded; in the morning the barge would be set adrift – not too early; when, as would inevitably happen, it was picked up by the police, the police would find a quantity of high explosive . . . they would scent both a cache and a catch; it would help to confuse the issue, draw some of the pressure away from the river if luck was with Mikhail. No point in Security agitating themselves too much about the river once the barge had been taken into custody. Attention might be switched to the Ecole Militaire, the Pompidou Centre which was also on the itinerary, or anywhere, it wouldn't matter.

Mikhail settled down for a series of cat-naps: he was too nervy at this stage for proper deep sleep. Stolnik slept well, the tired craftsman who had produced the goods and knew that, if all took an equal strain, it couldn't go wrong. Couldn't possibly. Little fat Annie curled into a ball and was soon asleep. Stolnik had said nothing about the girl having slid out to a disco without permission. The possibility of a leak would be worrying and since there was nothing to be done about that, there was no point in rocking the boat at this stage. Besides, Mikhail had a nasty temper; the only person who mattered to Mikhail was Mikhail – that, and his commitment to hitting back at the Soviets, a commitment shared wholeheartedly with Stolnik.

When morning came they breakfasted on rolls and butter and a thermos of coffee brought in the night before. There was little conversation; breakfast eaten, Mikhail walked up and down the warehouse, still nervy, a tic working in his long, dark face. Nicholas, watching from a dirty, cobwebbed window, looking out towards the river, reported groups of hippies along the quay. Mikhail joined him for a look. Tex? The American was a worry. There was no knowing . . . he might be in Paris, probably was. With the hippies. But the hippies could be coincidental. They were universal enough. With Nicholas and Stolnik he went over the schedule once again. The river boat was programmed to leave from the quay below the Eiffel Tower at 1430 hours; by approximately 1530 it should be coming down towards the Pont d'Austerlitz. The timing could not be exact; no-one could foretell the delays inseparable from such occasions. The Russians might be late in leaving the Ecole Militaire, so many things might crop up. But it could be relied upon that around 1530, possibly a little later, the boat would be somewhere off the Quai de la Rappée.

That would be enough.

The worry was Shard. Not, however, a very serious worry; Shard's knowledge was out of date. His mind would be filled with barges, barges laden with high explosive. Tex was in fact a bigger anxiety. As the morning wore on, more and more of the hippies arrived, thronging the quay beyond the warehouse, playing musical instruments, swaying, singing, waving their banners. It was an unsettling sight, bringing Tex into ever sharper focus.

Coincidence, or not?

He called little fat Annie over.

"Yes, Mikhail?" Breasts bouncing, she came across, smiling.

"Those hippies. Look through the window."

She did so, standing on a packing case to get a view.

"Do you recognise any of them? From the Ardèche commune?"

She looked for a long while. "No," she said at last. "There were so many there. It wouldn't be possible – "

"All right," Mikhail said. Little fat Annie got down. "Do you think Tex is with them?"

"I didn't see him. I do not know, Mikhail."

"All right," he said again, abruptly. Little fat Annie drifted away, humming a tune to herself, and sat on the floor. Mikhail paced, kept on checking his watch. A little after 1300 hours he began the assembly: the packing-case was brought out from its temporary storage behind the piled crates. Stolnik, carefully, almost lovingly doing the unpacking, watched Mikhail's face for admiration of his craftsmanship. But Mikhail did no more than nod his approval. After the unpacking, two stubby phials were brought from a box and given a last-minute check; and after this a small oblong leather-covered object was brought out from the packing-case. This when opened revealed knobs and dials and telescopic aerials.

At 1025 hours that morning the Paris river police made their find: down river, the barge laden with explosive. It had been towed away in much excitement. The terrorists' secret weapon? Nevertheless, with Shard's report of the strange detonators in mind, Paris, on an Establishment level, had still to be considered a time bomb. By some miracle of tight security and a harsh clamp-down on editors the Press had failed to publish any word about the threat; the French authorities were to be congratulated on that. If this had been London, there would have been a newsprint bonanza. Roberts-White dreaded to think what a panic-stricken Paris crowd would have been like. But, perhaps because Mrs Heffer had a loud voice, the rumour had spread that the British Prime Minister intended joining the Russians on the Seine and could doubtless be seen that afternoon, waving and smiling to the crowds along the banks while she conversed with the Russian Foreign Minister. Or possibly argued with him, which would be more interesting if more dangerous for world accord.

In the Elysée Palace, President Ligot shook with anger, dismay and astonishment but declined flatly to interfere. Madame Heffer was well enough aware of his views and he wished for no more argument; it was too fatiguing, especially so when you knew you were not going to win or even be listened to. What must be, must be. Metaphorically, he had washed his hands. One thing, however, worried him: had it been the right thing to do, after all – keeping the Press in such total ignorance, or more precisely forcing them not to publish such as they had gleaned via the flapping ears of their political correspondents? Had it? Should not the citizens of Paris have been warned, say, to keep well clear of the river? Madame Heffer would surely not deny them that! But when he conferred again with the Prefect of Police, the head of the GIGN and the Minister of State for Home Affairs plus the Mayor of Paris they all advised the same as they had advised earlier – that a warning would lead only to the panic already envisaged as an awful probability by Roberts-White. The whole conference

182

might be set at nought if there were riots; a good proportion of the Parisians would blame the Russians and there would be tremendous ill-feeling. The others would blame the British . . . no, it was better kept as secret as possible. Of course, it was such a pity about Madame Heffer, but . . .

"But if these people act even without their barge and there is an explosion or a shooting?" President Ligot asked.

"Ah . . ." The dignitaries took refuge in philosophical shrugs. That must not happen. The terrorists must be out-manoeuvred; there was one thing about the river: any attack if it still came there must surely be seen and avoiding action could and would be taken in time. It would not be like, say, a device planted in the Tour Montparnasse, the Eiffel Tower, or the Pompidou Centre, surreptitiously. The Seine was not a surreptitious thing. There was a very good chance, a hope of success. President Ligot had an idea they were all still thinking in terms of barges.

Mrs Heffer spent the morning dictating memoranda.

★   ★   ★

A very excellent lunch had been provided at the Ecole Militaire and the tour of the magnificent buildings had been most interesting. The Russian Foreign Minister had enjoyed it all; a fine chance to see something of the decadence of the West, all this pre-occupation with things past, with a military glory that for the West had gone forever. What, he asked himself, did Napoleon Buonaparte matter today?

Not a fig.

He was courteous nevertheless. He asked the right questions, expressed appropriate appreciation of fine furnishings and splendid paintings of ancient French battles. Napoleon's retreat from Moscow . . . a sore point still? Politely, the Minister offered no comment. Not even a solemn joke – the French were touchy, and Russians were not jokey people anyway. Kruschev, so many years ago, had often put his foot into Western susceptibilities because he thought he had a sense of humour . . . a crude, fat man.

Despite a brave face and a confident manner, the Minister

needed some Dutch courage at luncheon and he got it in plenty. Very fine wines . . . they helped. In the pit of the Minister's stomach anxiety rose like bile. But of course there were always threats. Men in high positions had to accept the price. And Mrs Heffer might very well be a protection. When these men saw her, they might retreat and await another opportunity. When he and his delegation were on their own . . . gulping down wine, the Minister's hand shook slightly. Two more full days yet to go. By keeping close to Mrs Heffer . . . but Russian delegations in the West always kept themselves to themselves, making use of a portable Iron Curtain, and the comrades in the Kremlin might misunderstand any deviation.

A little late, but not much, the Russian party left the Ecole Militaire at 1436 hours and were driven in a glittering motorcade to the Eiffel Tower along a street lined with somewhat morose-looking Parisians, only a wave and cheer here and there, which was disappointing. Off-loaded by the Eiffel Tower, the Minister and his party, completely surrounded the moment they left the cars by a strong posse of men in dark suits and hats and with hands already reached towards armpit bulges, went down to the Quai Branly. The boat was waiting not far from the Pont d'Iéna, and the British Prime Minister, arrived from her Embassy, was already aboard.

There was a cordial exchange of greetings. Mrs Heffer appeared unworried. So confident, like the British always were. She said, "Such a *lovely* day," in English. This was interpreted and the Minister agreed with a non-committal grunt. One had to be cautious. With British Prime Minister and Russian Foreign Minister sitting together on a bench beneath a scrubbed canvas awning, the pleasure craft came off the Quai Branly and heavily escorted in front, at the sides and in rear by police launches headed towards possible extinction.

17

There was a glimmer of light now.

At last!

Hope and relief rose in Hedge. Panting, very close to exhaustion, he squirmed forward. The constriction . . . he was moving on his stomach now, wormlike, pulling with extended arms, thrusting with his legs. His limbs felt as if they weighed a ton apiece. There was just about room. If he'd been a shade fatter . . . but that didn't bear thinking about. He'd have been stuck for ever to become a skeleton. No-one would have thought of digging up Paris to find him.

On a little more. He seemed to be climbing a little and after a while the light vanished and panic came down again. Hedge gave a sound of desperation. Perhaps it had been no more than a cruel mirage, even something in his imagination, or some physical manifestation of his intense desire to find anything to give him hope.

Down slightly now. Ah! There it was again – the light. Very small, very distant.

Hedge wormed on. At least there was no pursuit. Either the cellar wall had indeed become blocked by that earth fall, or Tex had had no intention of ever freeing him. The man was a monster.

★　　　★　　　★

Now it was ten minutes past three.

On the river the Prime Minister waved to right and left. Most of the spectators appeared to be the hippies. Few other people were risking getting caught up in the evil-smelling, largely dangerous-looking mob. The cheering that came across was derisive in the main although in one place the pleasure

185

boat went past a small group waving a Union flag with apparent gusto. There seemed to be a strong British contingent, or contingents: British banners waved, were flaunted, from various points along both banks. The usual stuff: MAKE LOVE NOT WAR, SEND DOWN A DOVE, PEACE MAN PEACE and so on. No less than four said HEFFER OUT. One, evidently composed by a wag, said HEFFER VESCENT OLD BAG. Since until this morning it had been only rumour that said the British Prime Minister would be aboard, it was reasonable to assume the anti-Heffer banners were fortuitous and had been meant for some other occasion. Likewise ARTHUR SCARGILL FOR PRESIDENT.

Mrs Heffer professed amusement. It was the best approach. Inside she was simply furious; a very bad impression would be given to the Soviet delegation. When, just beyond the Pont Neuf, that ponderous structure decorated with masks above its arches, another HEFFER OUT loomed up, the Prime Minister pointedly engaged the Russian Foreign Minister in animated conversation via the interpreter. Nothing political: was he impressed with Paris, did he like being on the river, did he not think the architecture of the Louvre to be superb? It was a stilted conversation. Mrs Heffer found the grim-faced Russian security men off-putting; and to a large extent they were obscuring the view – there were so many of them and they were hefty to a man. But never mind: what she could see past the torsos and between the legs was peaceful enough apart from the belligerent banners. Very peaceful, Paris in summer, and they were on the river. *Lovely.* Really, the threat seemed totally unreal, it could almost have been a hoax, a hippie hoax.

Also at 1510 hours Mikhail was standing ready in the warehouse behind the Quai de la Rappée. Stolnik's craftmanship was ready too: packed with thirty kilogrammes of plastic explosives, all connections made. The radio control had been tested and all was well. There could be no mistakes. Absolutely nothing could go wrong now.

Just one thing to be done: the assistance, in the penultimate stage, of a child was needed. Boy or girl, it didn't really matter. That was little fat Annie's job. And she was made for

186

it. She looked trustworthy, friendly, no vice. She had a happy face, the sort a child would co-operate with instantly when a game was mentioned.

"All right?" Mikhail asked, his voice taut.

"Yes, Mikhail. Is it now?"

"A few minutes yet. The boat's late. But no matter." He started pacing again, a caged lion.

★   ★   ★

"Here it comes," Tex said. He got to his feet; Shard and Eve did likewise. Tex, in the midst of his hippies, was confident enough to produce his gun from the ankle holster, but discreetly. He laid hold of Eve Brett, like a lover, and kept the gun in her side. Shard, looking back towards the Pont de Sully, saw the pleasure boat coming along with its VIP load.

Tex used a pair of binoculars, small ones that he'd brought from a shoulder bag. He said, "For Christ's sakes, it's right what the rumours said. She's there! Your Mrs Heffer."

Shard hadn't doubted the rumours that had run through the hippie mob. He thought of all the banners. Talk about sheer lunacy. He was helpless and knew it; and the actual sight of the Prime Minister was a much more present thing than rumour. But Tex seemed to have the answers and he had to be trusted now. Shard asked, "How are you going to stop this?"

"Just wait," Tex said. "And move – but fast. With me. In your own interest and Ma Heffer's, don't be bloody stupid and try anything on your own, right?"

He pushed through, towards the Pont d'Austerlitz. His personal squad moved with him, faces saying no-one come too close. There were no police around – not uniformed ones. Shard saw nothing that looked like a plain clothes man either. All the protection seemed to be on the river itself, the diving teams by the bridge supports, police river launches cruising ahead and astern of the VIP boat, crammed with armed men. Troops along the bridges themselves, no public admitted there. As the personal squad moved along they dived into their clothing and brought out pieces of dismembered gun. Efficiently Tex set them up: by the time they had gone twenty yards he had a telescopic-sighted, long range rifle, silenced, in his hands. As they moved, the hippies parted to let them through. It was an incredible thing to watch, to be part of. Tex was back, it seemed, to godhead. The hippies sensed his coming even with their backs turned. There was a curious sound, a kind of keening, a sort of vocal longing, a reaching out as if to God. Tex was really something to these people . . . Tex stopped in the lee of a wall, beneath the cover of a big tree that had survived the batter of the commercial port. He said, "Right over there." He pointed towards the Left Bank. "That's where it's going to happen. Any moment. Watch out."

He lifted his rifle ready, squinting along the sights, and waiting. His point of aim appeared to be the side of a warehouse behind the Quai de la Rappée.

★   ★   ★

The child was English, an appurtenance of an unmarried hippie mother. A little boy, six years old perhaps, chubby and friendly. Little fat Annie smiled at him; his mother wasn't taking much notice of him while she watched the approach of the VIPs. He wasn't lost but he was bored. Yes, he would like to sail a boat, but where was it?

"Not far," little fat Annie said. "In the warehouse – you see?"

"Yes. Where can I sail it from? The water's a long way down."

"There is a what do you call it, a slipway?" Little fat Annie took the boy's hand and led him to the warehouse. Stolnik took over from there. Out came the masterpiece, so beautifully made and never mind that within less than a minute now it would vanish for ever. He smiled at the child, patted his head with benevolence . . . the boy's expression was rapt. A wonderful scale model, a little over a metre in length, of an ocean liner, one of the old-timers, the *Ile de France*. With the boy trotting beside him, excellent cover – who would ever suspect a small boy, intent on sailing his boat? – Stolnik ferried the model on a trolley towards a derelict slipway only a matter of metres from the warehouse, a slipway where the Seine lapped shallowly. One middle-aged man, one eager, trusting child, and the small deadly detonators, one set into either bow of the model, tiny torpedoes that under radio control would take the side of the pleasure boat, set off the packed high explosive, and fragment the passengers.

As man and boy went off, little fat Annie, standing beside the warehouse, slowly raised both arms to the sun, a lascivious, almost an abandoned gesture of sun-worship. As she did so Tex, across the river, brought up his long range rifle, put the sights on Stolnik, then waited until the man had come back to the warehouse. As he did so, little fat Annie approached the door and called to someone inside.

"With luck," Tex said softly, "Mikhail'll come out. Then I'll – "

As he spoke he was spotted by one of the eagle-eyed Russians aboard the approaching pleasure boat. The sun had glinted . . . the Russian drew on the instant, an automatic rifle appearing as if by magic in his hands. He opened fire, fanned slightly, giving a spread. He got Tex. Tex collapsed to the ground in a heap, blood pouring. Shard bent. Tex could just speak, very low. "The boat, the model . . . get it for Christ's sakes!"

All around, there was panic, hippies pressing away, many being trodden underfoot. No-one except Shard and Tex had so much as noticed the model liner. No-one except Shard could now be relied on to assess its significance in time once it came out from the slipway. Which, any moment, it would.

No hesitation now. Shard fought his way through the mob of swaying, screaming hippies, using his fists to clear a path. There was no more firing. No-one was going to slaughter the hippies. The model emerged, swung to its starboard side, headed under its unseen controls towards the VIPs. Not seen yet; Shard dived. That was when the firing started

189

again, revolvers and rifles. Taking the river surface, he went deep.

★　　　★　　　★

"What a splendid model." Mrs Heffer stood up unsteadily for a better view. She was quite shaken: things had turned nasty. She had seen Tex fall, seen the ominous swaying of the crowd that took place afterwards. Yells, cries, incipient panic. It was better to concentrate on the model liner, show the world that she was unrattled. Then more shooting: a man in the water. What was he up to? Who was he? He was very lucky, Mrs Heffer assessed, to be alive, whoever he was.

Shard thought so too. God must be with him. Swimming submerged beneath peppered water he came up close to the model, reached out, tried to deflect it from its course. Partially he succeeded, but it came round again, bringing its torpedoes closer to the river boat.

The shooting stopped. Aboard one of the police launches an inspector had ticked over and had used his loud-hailer. That launch was now bearing down on Shard and the model.

"Any minute!" Shard shouted at the inspector. "Get the VIPs out of it!"

The launch turned and raced away, the inspector using his loud-hailer again, urgently, his voice cracking. Aboard the pleasure boat, the captain swung his wheel fast; the boat began to turn away. The model followed, tearing from Shard's grip, still under the radio control of its maker, Stolnik. Desperately Shard plunged on, got up alongside again, butted at the small hull and once again deflected it. This time it seemed to hesitate, made an uncertain movement . . . it could have been hit during the shooting, perhaps, was no longer able to make certain movements while it could still make others. It was a theory, anyway . . . Shard urged the lethal contraption across the river, anything to impede its progress towards the VIPs, who had to be given time to get clear away. If it blew, it blew – bloody bad luck . . . the hippies were already on the move, fighting, yelling, screaming to clear the banks on either side.

Nearer the Left Bank now. Then, as Shard got the thing

190

closer in, coming beneath the quay where there was an opening in the wall above, an opening more than half obscured by debris, a round hole like a big drain, or a sewer, a man appeared, staggering like a drunk, emerging from behind the debris. Dishevelled, filthy, uttering cries, blinded by the sudden bright sunlight, Hedge went clean over into the river. He came down flat across the model liner, sank, but clung to it like a limpet, the one possibly safe thing in a crazy, unkind world, and rode there, like a partly surfaced whale, as the panic spread along the river banks.

★   ★   ★

Shard went to see Hedge in hospital. He was recovering, and had already been visited by the Ambassador and by Mrs Heffer. Weakly, long-sufferingly, he asked Shard for any further news. He asked why the model hadn't blown up.

"A number of reasons," Shard answered. "Firstly, its controls had been interrupted by gunfire. Secondly and more importantly, little fat Annie had managed to withdraw the detonators while the others were occupied. Before it was launched. On Tex's instructions, that was." He paused. "You were never in any danger, you know. No-one was – except little fat Annie."

"Rubbish!" Hedge snapped. He saw the sardonic look in Shard's eye and changed his tack; but it wasn't fair to try to deny him his triumph. "What about those wretched men? Mikhail and – "

"In custody," Shard answered briefly. "Little fat Annie too."

"That stupid girl!"

"Not so stupid, Hedge. I've just told you – "

"Yes, yes, I know. And the man Tex?"

"Dead."

"Ah yes. The Russians. Just as well."

Shard looked down at obstinate petulance. No use trying to explain. Hedge never listened to explanations. But he was perking up. The Prime Minister had been congratulatory. If he, Hedge, hadn't sunk the model half Paris might be no longer in existence. Shard allowed him the exaggeration and didn't even make the point that his manifestation had been purely fortuitous. Hedge was now set for glory: not many people had ever saved a Prime Minister's life, and it seemed that Mrs Heffer had settled on him as her saviour. Whitehall and the Press would obviously follow suit. Hedge would preen as never before. For Shard and WDC Brett it was just part of the job. For Tex, without whom all would now be blood and diplomatic nightmare, it was just a would-be villain's death.